Power to Yield and other stories

Broken Eye Books is an independent press, here to bring you the odd, strange, and offbeat side of speculative fiction. Our stories tend to blend genres, highlighting the weird and blurring its boundaries with horror, sci-fi, and fantasy.

Support weird. Support indie.

brokeneyebooks.com
twitter.com/brokeneyebooks
facebook.com/brokeneyebooks
instagram.com/brokeneyebooks

POWER TO YIELD AND OTHER STORIES

"A seamless juxtaposition of intricate truths and bold fictions, these stories mesmerize." (**Nicky Drayden**, author of *Escaping Exodus* and *The Prey of Gods*)

"It's rare to find an author that truly deepens the speculative genre and human experience simultaneously but Takács is clearly one of them. E deftly unravels our preconceived notions of the self, society, culture, desire, power and the other and re-braids them in new insightful ways in each story. As you move through each richly-crafted story, you are challenged and transformed whether you realize it or not. This intimate yet expansive collection is not one to miss." (**Sloane Leong**, author of *Prism Stalker*, *Graveneye*, and *A Map to the Sun*)

"Bogi Takács's stories never fail to awe with their breadth and depth of thought, precise prose, and fascinating characters. In *Power to Yield and Other Stories*, Takács reveals emself to be a masterful gardener, cultivating these tales of science and magic, of immigrants and exiles, of deep loss and abiding hope. Whether you're new to eir work or know it well, this collection will welcome you, for it is expertly tended and blooming with glorious sights, its roots stretching across cultures, bodies, worlds, and ages." (**Izzy Wasserstein**, author of *All the Hometowns You Can't Stay Away From*)

"['Power to Yield'] is a fascinating take on aspects of power, history, personal obsession, and sadism, the latter all taking place within an asexual framework that removes those questions from their normal sexual-overtone-laden context." (**Karen Burnham**, *Locus Magazine*)

"['Power to Yield'] is laced with pain and with the fractured lines of a people stitched together from trauma and systemic abuse, who come together out of necessity and the need for freedom to make something powerful and beautiful. [...] And it's a lovely, rending read that I definitely recommend people check out immediately!" (**Charles Payseur**, *Quick Sip Reviews*)

Power to Yield and other stories

BOGI TAKÁCS

POWER TO YIELD AND OTHER STORIES
by BOGI TAKÁCS

Published by
Broken Eye Books
www.brokeneyebooks.com

Content notices and publication history of individual
stories can be found at the end of this volume.

978-1-940372-66-2 (trade paperback)
978-1-940372-67-9 (hardcover)

TABLE OF CONTENTS

FOREWORD

OW MANY DIFFERENT MINDS CAN THERE BE IN THE WORLD? How can information pass from one mind to another when we're all so different? What does it cost us to breach the divides that make such communication difficult—and what does it cost when we refuse to try?

If these are the questions that interest you, then allow me to introduce Bogi Takács.

Bogi and I have been friends and colleagues since the dark ages of LiveJournal—2010, I think? The internet moves fast enough that some of the details are lost in the caverns of time. I've known em since before either of us had a professional-level story sale or a book out—also before e moved from Hungary to the US. In all that time, we've never met in person. This is the paradox of the internet, bringing people together across impossible distances while in other ways keeping them just as far apart.

What's always impressed me about Bogi is the flexibility of eir mind, leaping into the guises of aliens, machines, spiritual beings, plants, animals, monsters, and humans alike. Bogi is a multiply neurodivergent, multiply disabled, queer, trans, intersex, Jewish immigrant from a non-Anglo country. If you think that living at the confluence of all these axes of marginalization might require some creative code-switching, you are correct. Autistic people get told that we can't imagine other people's minds, but everything in Bogi's work is perspective-taking, usually several perspectives at once, usually including some perspectives so unusual that others wouldn't think of them at all.

These perspectives are significantly different from each other. The characters are constantly trying to communicate across impossible gulfs of difference—whether those differences are science fictional or the results of privileges and marginalizations that humans have always had. In "The Ladybug, in Flight," a member of a space hive mind speaks to a child, who may be the only survivor of a spaceship disaster whose seriousness the hive mind isn't quite equipped to understand. In "Four-Point Affective Calibration," a marginalized narrator tries to have their emotions read by a machine learning system and wonders if the way they process emotions is normative enough for the machine. In "And I Entreated," a Jewish woman is transformed into a houseplant and tries, with increasing frustration, to communicate with her family through a telepathic translator who is only somewhat reliable. In "Volatile Patterns," a group of people appropriate another culture's magical designs into their clothing, only to reproduce the designs incorrectly and with disastrous results. In "The 1st Interspecies Solidarity Fair and Parade," humans and aliens are trying to collaborate in a post-apocalyptic world—but the difficulty of getting different groups of humans to cooperate proves almost as great as the difficulty of talking to the aliens. When the groups do come together, it's a hilariously chaotic, joyful mess.

There is a lot of pain in this collection, but also a lot of playfulness and a lot of awareness of more than one kind of power differential. Characters with contrasting forms of neurodivergence try to adjust their approaches, so they can work together. Jewish families navigate nuanced differences in their individual approaches to religion and gender while also navigating the development of AI and telepathy or being turned into a houseplant. In "A Technical Term, Like Privilege" a person with inborn magical talent is turned away from a community of revolutionaries, on grounds that their magic makes them privileged—(I winced in recognition so hard at this scene that I had to take a break)—but the reality of what their magic does for them is more complicated and grimmer, and they find a way to use it for a revolution of their own.

While there is a lot of successful work to bridge divides, some can't be bridged—especially those created by bigotry and cruelty, as in "On Good Friday the Raven Washes Its Young," or by willful dismissiveness. When human society cannot be endured, the characters facing these divides often ally themselves with aliens or other powerful presences. Or they turn into plants for safety, as in "Folded into Tendril and Leaf," only to find that something of the plant way of being stays with them permanently. "Power to Yield" itself is in some sense a story about this kind of alliance, with Aramīn—distrusted by everyone due to his neurotype—finding meaning in the inhuman System he maintains. These inhuman presences generally aren't sinister, though there's always a human somewhere who has reason to view them that way. They are just different and not to be ignored.

I should talk a little more about that title story, which is the longest and last in the collection. (Though there'll be a few spoilers, so if you'd rather not have them, you can skip the rest of this foreword.) It's a challenging but fascinating novella, in which the magical planet Eren—a setting Bogi has written about before, here and elsewhere—would be unlivable, full of monsters and uncontrollable expressions of magic, if not for the System that keeps it in order. The System is designed by Aramīn, who is a Falconer—a neurotype that seems to resemble antisocial personality disorder. He has little innate sense of morality, but adheres strictly to moral rules that he's consciously learned, knowing no one will forgive him for a misstep. A young autistic woman named Oyārun develops a special interest in Aramīn, eventually meeting him and volunteering to participate in the System herself. Aramīn worries that her special interest compromises her ability to consent, but he agrees.

It turns out that magically talented volunteers maintain the System through sadomasochistic practices that allow them to join their intelligence to a structure larger than themselves. It's an ecstatic experience, and occasionally a terrible one; it's also addictive. In a way, the System is the ultimate form of connection: it not only keeps Eren physically safe but also holds all the community's knowledge, all their networks, and all their ways of communicating with each other. Neither character, as their relationship develops, is portrayed as a blameless victim or a monster. Both of them are trying to balance their inherent interests and the needs of the community, knowing that these efforts will always be questioned and always flawed.

Maybe there's never a form of communication that is ever not flawed, that doesn't twist someone's meaning or leave someone out, by mistake or by design.

Maybe it's morally incumbent upon us to keep communicating anyway. Or maybe it's not moral at all, but merely what we need to do to survive.

To judge for yourself, turn the page.

—Ada Hoffmann (July, 2023)

FOUR-POINT AFFECTIVE CALIBRATION

Prompt: Anger

OF COURSE, I CAN BE ANGRY.

But I wear a headscarf. The moment I'm angry, you put me in your mental box labeled "TERRORIST" in neat, tidy small capitals. You store me under "POTENTIAL DANGER" in the warehouse of your mind.

When I cross the parking lot to the grocery store, sometimes people hit the gas, not the brakes. And this is a university town, supposedly liberal—or is it?

I'm not a Muslim, but it's not like most people around here can spot the difference. I allow you to guess my religion, my level of observance, my gender. You will probably guess wrong.

Let's start over. I can be angry, but I won't.

I won't because it would not have gotten me out of secondary screening, immigration detention, hostile interrogation, and all the other abstract concepts that need at least two words to describe. I lived to learn.

But you know? Maybe I'm not angry because I'm not.

You expect me to be angry—or at least be silent but simmering with rage. And sure, I can work myself up to it. But right now, I'm mostly just annoyed, sitting here under the helmet and asked to contemplate various emotions supposedly basic, supposedly universal across cultures. I have my doubts about this last part.

I hope next up is sadness because thinking about anger makes me sad.

Prompt: Sadness

I wish my thoughts were tidier. A complete stranger will be examining these transcripts. I keep on going off on tangents.

I have a succulent on my living room table that keeps on trying to grow out of its pot and downward, forming a fringe of thick green bundles. But its branches are not strong enough to support their own weight, and they keep breaking off, wasting away. The plant does not give up, and I water it dutifully, try to rotate it so that it occupies various positions with respect to the north-facing window, the evanescent sunlight.

It only wants to grow downward, toward certain harm.

This is not a metaphor; this is straight-up life. Plants have personalities—the balsam gourd in the office is feisty, rapidly growing tendrils toward all the other pots, seeking to reach out and tickle. Possibly smother.

Maybe you chose me for this task because I'm so observant.

Is this enough for sadness? Can I get a different one? Impatience is not a basic emotion, I am told.

[Pause]

Disgust is apparently a subcategory of anger, but I really don't want to redo that segment. They should've briefed me first—this is not my field, and I only know about Ekman's six basic emotions from undergrad. Happiness, surprise, fear, anger, sadness, disgust. People refine their models all the time.

I threw out all my models—and again and again. *Extraterrestrial communication* is also an abstract concept that needs two words to describe. It doesn't sound much friendlier than *hostile interrogation*.

Prompt: Fear/Surprise

Fear and surprise fall under the same heading, emotions evoked by "fast-approaching danger." I'm trying to scrape my brain for citations: Jack et al., I don't remember the year.

I didn't sleep through the initial briefing; I was just so anxious that nothing they said registered. Sure, I can tell you about the amygdala, fear response, interactions with short-term memory. It's not really an excuse though. Does it matter? I feel like I'm in my comprehensive exams again, being interrogated by my committee, even though it's just my thoughts being transcribed. Even though this is just the calibration phase.

I feel like I am looking at the immigration officer again.

Deep breath. I can upset myself with great alacrity and skill.

The research team think aliens will probably not understand the substance of my thoughts as much as the underlying emotions—at least at first. Everything needs to be precisely calibrated.

Am I too scatterbrained? I'm told that everyone has messy transcripts. Mine feel worse. I'm put on the spot. There are plenty of backup people standing by if my calibration fails, if the factors won't converge—if, if. Plenty of people to take my spot.

Who wants the person in the headscarf? They made me take it off to put on the helmet, they made me take it off on the border, even for my driver's license, my ridiculous student ID photo, my clip-on work ID stating my name and my surprisingly senior position. It's not the right name either, but at least, it doesn't have a gender marker, and it's not like people can spell my name anyway.

In the past two decades in this country, I have amassed a variety of ID photos with uncovered-head me. Maybe I should make an installation. Very artistic.

I'm supposed to produce fear and surprise on command, not anger. I don't think my emotions segment into four neat categories. Boxes in the warehouse. I can try again—I do think I had the fear component. As for surprise, I would need to be surprised.

When I got this assignment, I was surprised.

It made me rethink that moment back over a decade ago in undergrad when in tears I confessed my diagnosis to my biostatistics professor, when he dragged me to Disability Services. If I'd stayed in my country of origin—I refuse to say home country, this is my home country now—if I'd stayed, I would never have experienced that moment. Disability Services wasn't particularly a thing back there. I'm told now it's different.

Surprise. Focus. When I'm nervous, I fidget, constantly readjusting my clothes, my scarf—and I'm clumsy, so I sometimes pull it off my head altogether. I've never seen anyone else do that, but most of the other autistic people I know are staunch atheists. Secular people are horrified on my behalf, and I feel embarrassed, but I don't think [uninterpretable] minds much—after all, [uninterpretable] is supposedly all-knowing and [uninterpretable].

I pull at my clothes and [uninterpretable] [uninterpretable] my fingers even now, but I'm reprimanded that this produces motion artifacts.

I really want to talk to aliens, so I try to sit still. Just one more emotion to go.

Prompt: Happiness

I know why they saved happiness for last—it's because of the priming effects. If I finish with happiness, I will remain a bit happier for a little while. They didn't tell me about this, but I do work with human participants in my own line of research.

I'm glad I transitioned from purely quantitative to mixed-methods. Extraterrestrial communication needs all the methods we can throw at it. Of course, it's my quantitative-minded colleagues who will read the transcripts. Stop with those thoughts, I don't want to lose my job. Am I expected to think of sex? I generally don't think of sex.

Happiness. Happiness is a vast spacecraft, reminiscent of alien-invasion movies but accompanied by a feeling of elation and relief. Happiness is change.

I'm sure the people in the lab next door chose me for this assignment because they have these ridiculous stereotypes that being neuroatypical makes me better at understanding aliens. But you know, one tiny part of that is true: I want to talk to aliens because I'm fed up with humans sometimes. When I was compared to space aliens as a kid, I probably internalized the wrong message—I decided that aliens must be really cool.

Happiness is love. Happiness is change and aliens are change and love is aliens—I move along the chain of associations. I don't care about formal logic. Love is aliens.

They want to talk. Not shoot, destroy, evaporate, invade—they want to talk. I want to talk. They don't know how. We're working on it.

I used to be an alien—of a different kind: a resident alien, and before that, a non-resident. And inside me, a warm feeling bubbles up as I'm told that the calibration has finished, concluded, I am ready, I have passed.

I know with the certainty of joy that I can help the newcomers with settling in.

AN ERRANT HOLY SPARK

I HAVE NEVER BEEN KIDNAPPED BEFORE.

This is the first time I'm threatened with a firearm, dragged into an unmarked white van, deposited into a windowless basement after a long drive. All the standard steps of kidnapping, played out one after another.

A bullet to the head would destroy me just the same as it would kill you. I'm not going to risk it.

I know that gaze—you are trying to catch me out. You watch me closely to find those moments where I betray my supposedly true nature. You listen to the slightest changes in my tone of voice.

You stare like this at trans people to guess their birth assignment or confirm it to yourself. You frown as you read articles by people with obviously foreign names, trying to pinpoint each turn of phrase that would mark the writer as a non-native speaker, to find an expression that would be sufficiently un-American. But when you stare at *me*, you are trying to prove to yourself that I'm really artificial—a construct, a robot, what have you.

The underlying concept is the same: you're trying to find the telltale signs that would enable you to exclude me from the human condition. And you need to do this in order to be able to do your job.

Are you interrogating me for the government? I work *for* the government. Or is this some clandestine, black-ops faction, operating largely without oversight? Is this about the extraterrestrials, again?

It has to be—otherwise why would you ask about my family?

I have two mothers and another parent.

This is a trap: if I minutely, meticulously explain my feelings, this in itself will prove their artificial nature to you. If I don't bother, you will simply disregard their existence.

I cannot win, so I might as well talk. It is a form of stalling, after all.

Shoshana Cahane is my designer. I call her Mom. I think of her as Mother, because I feel *Mom* doesn't express enough deference. Saying *Mother* out loud would feel too formal, even though it rings right to me. She is my mother, but she is also my designer, which is a different position somehow.

In my first memory of her, I'm sitting in her car, looking at a small glass vial filled with tiny white snail shells. The doors are open, the AC not on. It is the heat of summer, and everything has that vaguely unreal feel in the blatant glare of sunlight. I stare at the shells and think the vial was a gift from someone who left. I realize I have memories that stretch back quite far. I remember being given the vial, and I know it is now mine.

Mother sits down next to me and leans toward me to ask what's on my mind. Her thick, dark curls fall in front of her round face, but I know she's smiling at me. I know even without looking. I tell her about my memories, and she is pleased.

There is a strange metacognitive twist here: I no longer remember the memories I told her about.

I know you want to hear about how Dani Blumenfeld can talk to the extraterrestrials. I suppose you also want to hear about the secret of teleportation. But you'll need to be patient. We are all related.

Nurit Tzipora Cahane is my developmental model: in a sense, my mother almost as much as Mother is. I call her Tzipi. She is two years older than me.

I read about Vygotsky's zone of proximal development in one of Mother's books—when I was still in kindergarten but when I could already read. One can divide all possible human activities into three sets: some the child can do, some the child cannot do at all, and the zone of proximal development. This third set holds the activities that are possible through the aid of another human. To help children learn, you need to provide activities that fall into this zone.

Hence, Tzipi.

Mother tells other people Tzipi is my sister—and certainly older siblings can provide great potential for learning. But with Tzipi, it is more than that. I *am* her, in a sense. She was my initial template.

My first iteration has a set of four clumsy actuators connected to a central globe, the actuators further subdivided.

It is a model: a model of humans. A model of Tzipi specifically. All models are wrong.

My second iteration, I develop myself: rolling after Tzipi, my actuators held out in parallel, my sensors alert to every little change.

Mother is in her office, working.

Tzipi picks me up with great difficulty and drops me. I'm shaped like a ball, but I don't bounce.

I don't feel pain yet.

I can see the incredulity on your face. Surely you weren't a heavy metallic ball with spokes sticking out?

No, my casing was made of polypropylene.

And why is your first memory of Tzipi so much earlier than that of your mother?

Mother was always in her office.

My first memory of Dani is even later. I was five. Human-shaped. Cognitively much ahead of my chronological age. At that point, Tzipi already treated me like an older sister.

I was crawling under the long dinner table with her—the tablecloth almost to the floor, making a giant caterpillar of a tent. All the numerous guests had already dispersed, except for Dani, Mother's younger sibling, who would stay with us for the holiday starting the following night.

We didn't notice Dani. We were engrossed in our make-believe scheme in which the caterpillar-tent was a spaceship, and we were its operators. I had read about this in a book and would lecture Tzipi on the proper procedures when she only wanted to pretend to press buttons and squeal in delight as we imitated a launch.

We got to the end of the table only to see a pair of legs in slacks, feet in plastic slippers. We scurried back but did not dare exit the imagined safety of our spaceship. We were stuck in the middle as the person began to sing or chant, an entirely unfathomable melody, rapid and intricate. A voice assertive yet light.

I had heard some of the guests speak this language—and also Mother on occasion when she was making work calls—and I knew it was Hebrew. But ours was a secular household, where even the big Passover gathering of relatives and friends was on the day before Passover simply because it was more convenient. They could then go to a real seder the next day, a real holiday celebration. I had never before heard anyone pray, had no inkling of how it sounded.

We crouched under the table, entirely motionless and spellbound, until the chanting ended.

"You can come out now," the person yelled to us in cheerful English still accented with the tones of prayer. "Have you ever been to a Passover Seder?"

We shook our heads.

"Shoshi, eh? You're her kids, right?"

We nodded.

"If no one else here will do a seder for you, I will."

I looked at them. I did not have to guess their pronouns because they were wearing a pronoun badge. They were short where Mother was tall, so light-skinned it was hard to believe the two of them were relatives, and they were wearing an intricately tied scarf.

Mother always tried to look "American," as she put it. Dani looked American and wore all this ethnic clothing. I could not figure this out for years.

Mother made me.

Tzipi formed me.

But it was Dani who taught me Torah.

I was seven. Starting elementary school. Hopelessly ahead, but Mother insisted on enrolling—for the social experience, she said.

The kids teased me cruelly, but I supposed that in itself was the social experience I needed to acquire. I had not yet begun to protest.

Dani was visiting again—for the High Holidays this time. I had demanded their presence. Cried, not like Tzipi would but with my own entirely earnest tears. Mother gave in, and Dani arrived. At that point, I'd already understood Dani was the odd one out, the only one in an otherwise conventional family of mostly French Jews of Hungarian and Slovakian origin.

Mother was the other odd one out, the one who moved to the United States for grad school and threw herself into machine learning with abandon. Single-parenting. Ploughing forward. As she would say: "I'm not taking any crap from anyone."

Mother would tell me about the world: how money worked, why highways and helicopters existed, why her family moved from Eastern Europe to Paris, a neighborhood where many other Jews were from North Africa. She told me about colonies and occupations, she told me about quasi-mythical governesses from centuries ago, and she showed me La Défense on the internet.

But Dani would answer questions that Mother would evade.

Dani grinned at me. Instead of the scarf, this time they were wearing a baseball hat with the colors of a team entirely unknown to me.

When I could finally find myself alone with them, I asked.

"Dani, why do I have a soul?"

Everyone else would have responded, Do *you have a soul?*

Dani just grinned again, their face angular where Mother's was soft. "I don't know. Hashem wants you to have one, so there you have it."

Dani always used the Hebrew name for G-d. I imitated them. "Why does Hashem want me to have a soul?" I asked.

"Hmmmmm." Dani furrowed their brow. "I would say you are a suitable vessel for it?"

"Yes, but Mother designed me and made me. It's not"—I groped for words that didn't exist—"natural? It's artificial? I didn't just . . . grow?"

"You grew all right. You're bigger every time I see you!" Dani laughed.

I shrugged, conceding the point. I did grow. I developed. Mostly due to processes not accessible to my conscious awareness, but wasn't that true of everyone?

"Still, I don't think it matters," they continued after a while. "You had what it takes to host a holy spark, and Hashem provided and continues to provide a holy spark."

I *felt* that way, but I also felt the need to be defiant. I was inching toward adolescence even while the world thought I was a child. "But why do you believe that? Didn't they throw you out of synagogue?"

Mother had said that. And I shouldn't have flung it back in anyone's face. But Dani simply shrugged. "I was thrown out of an Orthodox synagogue, not all of Judaism itself. That would be quite a feat!"

"So are you Reform now?" Mother would not explain about denominations, so I had looked them up online, well in advance of this conversation.

"I'm too Orthodox still to be Reform," Dani laughed. "Too trans to be Orthodox, at least in their eyes. And I believe because it feels right."

I didn't have any arguments against that.

When did Mother first talk to me about the extraterrestrials?

I came home from school. There was a wide black streak on my red pullover where one of the boys had thought it good to attack me with permanent marker. My entire existence felt askew.

"You and the younger kids like you are even more important now," Mother said. "You can travel to space."

I thought I was important because I had a holy spark inside me, but I didn't say that.

Dani had told me that some of the Chasidim believed that holy sparks were scattered all across Creation, and it was their task to gather them together by performing good deeds.

I really liked this. I was an errant spark that had found its way to a suitable vessel.

"You can withstand hard radiation," Mother said.

The two of us huddled together on the lower bunk of our bunk bed. We had hung a checkered blanket to cover the opening. We'd closed the door, but we still felt an additional need for privacy.

Tzipi whispered, "When I grow up, I want to learn to talk to the aliens."

I shook my head. "It doesn't work like that. You can either talk to them, or you can't at all."

"Have you ever tried?"

Of course not. We'd never seen an extraterrestrial.

Tzipi went on, her voice rising until it was more of a stage whisper. "I heard Dani can talk to the aliens. And it runs in families."

No one had told me that about Dani. I felt slighted.

"Do you think Mother can talk to the aliens too?" I asked Tzipi. She giggled. Mother didn't really like talking to anyone, though she made an exception for us. She always seemed more at ease with us than with the adults. And I could understand that about me—after all, she had designed me, but Tzipi had come to the world through entirely conventional means.

"Do you think I can talk to the aliens too?" I whispered after she'd stopped giggling.

"You don't have an organic brain," she said, suddenly serious.

I felt like I was encroaching on her territory.

"Do I have to have an organic brain?" I asked.

"Isn't that how telepathy works?" She immediately posed a question to my question, and I had no answer.

I did try to tell myself that no one knew how telepathy worked.

Dani stayed over. Not for a few days, not for the holidays—permanently.

Dani was assigned to Extraterrestrial Communication Center Three. The Center, through a twist of fate, was almost in our backyard. It was easier for Dani to just move in with us instead of bunking in some Brutalist government dorm.

It wasn't precisely fate though, I felt. It was hashgacha pratit: divine providence. I had many more questions for Dani, and now I could pose them.

"Why do you have scratches on your face?" I asked.

Dani explained the extraterrestrials were trying to work with the humans, but it didn't always work out right.

"Can you tell what I'm thinking?" I asked.

"I have a vague impression," they said.

"What does it mean that you can sense my thoughts?"

"It means that you have thoughts. But I knew that already."

I was confused. Weren't my thoughts purely algorithmic? I had always assumed so, only that the algorithm was so complex as to be unfathomable. Did the execution of an algorithm, however complex, qualify as a thought?

This I could ask of Mother. I dashed out of the room, across the narrow corridor, looking for her.

I almost bumped into her around the corner. She steadied me even though she knew I did not need to be steadied. I had an excellent sense of balance.

I explained between gasps, between tears. Come face to face with existential fear.

"Your mind has a stochastic component," she said.

Dani caught up to us. They said, "Doesn't everyone's?"

"Well," Mother sounded bitter all of a sudden, "you're the expert on that."

"Can you talk to the aliens?" I finally cornered Mother.

I know this is the part you want to hear—one of them, anyway.

Mother said, "It's *extraterrestrials*. And I'm too busy working on my own projects."

I could tell she was evading the question.

"Do you think I could talk to the, the extraterrestrials?"

She raised her head and flicked a display out of the way. She stared at me as if suddenly seeing me anew, as if I'd said something entirely unexpected for the first time in my life.

"Well," she said, "it might be worth a try."

You know this situation is entirely pointless? Extraterrestrials can teleport. But you say, no one could ever convince them to do it on demand, and what should I do but concede that point?

It is definitely not easy to talk to them.

The scars on Dani's face were filled with glittering streaks of blue and yellow, like stained glass. Dani seemed unsteady, their head wavering slightly.

"We are trying very hard to work together," they explained as we were on our way to the Center. "It is very difficult. They're trying very hard, and we're trying very hard too. I'm sorry I'm repeating myself. I'm just very tired."

I took hold of their hand, and this seemed to help them focus on the here and the now. But I felt like I was drifting away into a realm of emptiness and anxiety. Was I really doing this just to one-up Tzipi? To show my brain was as good as organic?

I didn't feel the need to demonstrate to myself that I had a soul. I knew it with unassailable certainty.

The Hebrew word *emuna* is usually translated into English as "faith." But it means something more like firmness. Steadfastness. Safety. It carries an entirely different set of connotations from the Christian *faith*.

Dani began to whistle a melody, a tune that brought into my mind the matching words. *Ani maamin b'emuna shleima . . .* I believe with perfect faith, or rather, I believe with complete firmness . . . *b'viat haMashiach, ani maamin.* In the coming of the Messiah.

The ETs were here. But it did not feel like the end times. It felt like the beginning of something new.

The extraterrestrials were tall, their substance as if made of colorful glass. They had globular segments and thin, reedlike segments, but no two individuals had the same spatial configuration—though my sample size was small. I only saw five of them in the room, and none other in the entire building complex.

They all seemed to want me near them—not in a pushy way, more like a request, but one that was formed without words and entirely through gesture. One of them looked especially friendly and shook their dark-blue globes eagerly at me, like a string rattling.

I inched closer, afraid I'd slip on the oddly textured floor. I had on a pair of slippers that I really liked: they were a comfortable, warm dun with large red hearts applied to the front. But their soles were mostly flat, and they squeaked as I hesitated.

The ETs wanted to show me something, and I was curious. I looked back at Mother and Dani. Mother looked uncomfortable, but she smiled at me. Dani grinned too. Mother nodded, and that was it: I decided to go.

I followed the ETs into a smaller side room, with what seemed like a giant glass mushroom in the middle. It was colored in broad swipes of red, blue, and orange, and it glowed from within. I put a hand on it, and a piece of it jumped out, like a handle. I turned it this way and that, and the top of the mushroom unfolded like a flower with sharp, narrow petals. It reminded me of the scratches on Dani's face and then the way they were filled in with a substance resembling colored glass.

I had no idea what was going on, but the ETs were encouraged. We went back out into the larger room. The one with the dark-blue globes stood in front of Dani for a moment and then turned around and returned to the group.

"I told you they can talk to her," Dani told Mother.

I was confused. "They didn't talk to me. They just . . . pointed and gestured."

Dani scratched their head under the baseball cap. "That's how you perceive their communication. It's a bit different with everyone. They do not actually have gestures."

This didn't make any sense to me. "Maybe I can just . . . extract the information better. Machine learning is great for these kinds of tasks." I had heard that exact sentence from many other people. Never from Mother though.

She shook her head vehemently, her curls flying. "There is no information to extract. They do not use gesture to communicate. It seems that way to you because your mind tries to fit the information into pre-existent channels."

Dani shrugged. "I see pictures."

Mother said, "I hear screeching noise." She grimaced. "I do *not* like screeching noise. I need to keep myself busy, or they'll drag me away to spend my time talking to the extraterrestrials."

I felt bad about all the times I was resentful of her long hours, of her secluding herself in her office. Not so many people could talk to the ETs. She had to have gone to great lengths to justify her other work. Then again, she was famous—famous in the way few scientists get to be famous.

She also spent a lot of effort isolating me and Tzipi from the media hubbub.

I suddenly had a sinking feeling. What if the government would want to keep *me* here? Who would notice *my* absence, besides my family?

Mother frowned. Did she hear *my* thoughts as screeching noise too? She did seem to understand my fear.

Dani as well. "You can come visit any time you want," they said. "There's plenty to do. But you should work on growing up first before you commit to such a major task. At least, that's what the ETs think."

That sounded reassuring. That felt reassuring. And that in itself gave me pause.

Had I always been aware of people's thoughts, just interpreted them as gesture? Assumed I was doing conventional theory-of-mind inferencing? I'd read Mother's papers and much more besides.

This would account for at least some of my rapid development. Weren't I developing faster than most of the other kids built by other researchers?

We walked home in silence. I could not put my emotions into words.

I'm dismayed you don't ask about Three-Blue-Upside. How we ended up talking, working together, learning from each other. The ETs want to learn from us just as much as we do from them; our knowledge of the world has developed on entirely different paths, and the slightest detail can shed light on longstanding mysteries.

Mathematics is difficult to explain, save for certain branches of geometry and topology.

But you don't ask about that. You don't ask about how we taught each other to laugh in the other's way, how I once spent an entire afternoon trying to get across why humans find cats appealing, all the frustration and frustration and the pure moments of joy.

You only ask about my family. You ask about me.

I expected this. I'm still disappointed.

I realized very fast that Tzipi could probably also communicate with the ETs. She was my developmental model after all, not Mother. But Mother probably wanted to protect her from a future that would otherwise prove to be her only future, so she somehow managed to avoid taking her to the Center. Did Mother have to ask for favors? How long would those favors last? What would Tzipi do as an adult? Were the ETs here to stay? What did they want? There were too many uncertainties.

As for my future, who could tell? It was an experiment, albeit one in naturalistic conditions. Mother probably thought I could provide an interesting answer to a longstanding dilemma.

No, not about the nature of the soul.

I know that's why I'm here.

I know that's why you kidnapped me.

I know that mother somehow, entirely tangentially to her main research project, invented artificial telepathy.

I know she doesn't know how it happened.

No, I don't know how it happened either. I don't have such fine-grained insight into my development. I wouldn't be able to focus on anything if I had any awareness of how my individual components worked together. Can you isolate the activity of each of your own neurons?

I don't know why I can understand ETs as much as anyone can.

I'm sorry to disappoint. You knew it was coming. You can interrogate me all you like.

Reverse-engineering my mind would be no easier than reverse-engineering yours. It grew with a process comparable to yours.

I was designed, inasmuch as the processes that produced me were designed. Their outcome was not predictable. You cannot take me apart to see how I was built. My mind is a black box like yours. My brain is artificial, but its components do not have clearly separable function.

I know you would still try. And that's why *I* am here. I am here to gather evidence.

You think I would be here a moment longer than necessary?

I could leave a message saying, "Coercing people is wrong." Something straightforward and hard to swallow exactly because it's so self-evident.

I know one of your arguments would be that I'm not a person.

It's good that I have a sister. And thanks to mother's efforts, the media has no recent pictures of us.

And if you still think—with mother, Dani, Tzipi, and all of us together—we haven't managed to learn from the ETs how to teleport, think again.

Think fast before the air pops with displaced matter, a string of blue globes peeking out and then a human head—never figured out those team colors on the cap. Before all of us come streaming out of nowhere. Before your weapons stop working and your brains shudder in confusion.

Think fast before I'm gone.

AND I ENTREATED

REACHED THAT STAGE REPORTED BY JEWISH PARENTS WORLDWIDE where you know your kid's bar mitzvah portion inside and out, forwards, backwards. Except I was a houseplant.

It was supposed to be temporary. I had been painstakingly transformed into a giant potted plant with waxy leaves. And I could not name the species even if you threatened to tear out my stalks, but it was one of those kinds popular as office decoration throughout Alliance space and beyond. Certainly, my size suited an executive suite. Then, I was ceremoniously loaded onto a pallet and deposited in Head Councilor Liesethan's office as a gift from the Alliance. After that, my potting soil was poked and prodded for listening devices by Liesethan's staff, my leaves inspected, and so on. When they were satisfied that I did not carry anything untoward, and I was relaxed that I would finally be left to gather intelligence on Liesethan's most private conversations, they rolled me out into the corridor.

I spent two weeks in an alcove by his door, hearing only the tail ends of his negotiations as he was trying to cajole his country and especially his fellow councilmembers into joining the Alliance. It was frustrating to say the least, but as an officer of Alliance Intelligence, I was used to frustration.

I was not used to what came next: the administrator telling me that they were "very sorry, truly," that they did not have any shapechangers to spare with the Haisin crisis flaring up again and could I just wait for a day or two to be transformed to my usual shape.

My family did not expect me to return as a houseplant, but my husband Doron deposited me in our kid's bedroom, *Just until the Alliance finally gets off their collective behinds, dear.* He was in Counterintelligence and had seen his share of mishaps. Gil had promised to "cheer me up" and "provide me company" during Doron's long work hours, and Gil's bedroom was also larger than ours. There was little room on the station—it was home, yes, but a very squished-together sort of home. Cozy and heimish, on a good day; cramped and aggravating on a bad day. In Gil's room, I could temporarily stand in a corner, at least.

A day became two became a week and then two. Gil was preparing for their bar mitzvah, and I hoped I would not have to be dragged to the synagogue on a pallet. Their Torah portion was VaEtchanan, "And I Entreated." "And I Pleaded," in some translations. They practiced it endlessly, probably to procrastinate from schoolwork. Or were they worried about the sound of their voice? After a few thousand repetitions—at least that was how it had felt to me—I was ready to plead and entreat and beg.

I loved Gil with all my heart. But they were mostly in school or sitting at their desk, lying on their bed, nervously twirling their brown curls. Sometimes they put on very loud music that made my leaves shake and my sight blur. The only time they ever said anything out loud was when they were reciting their Torah reading or when they said goodnight to me before bed. I expected them to monologue at me, but I could not respond, and thus, they wouldn't. Maybe they felt too self-conscious about that.

These were the most frustrating two weeks of my life. At least I could see with my leaves, stare at Gil's assorted knickknacks on their shelves. I didn't know how that worked and did not want to contemplate it. I just wanted to be human-shaped again.

"But beware and watch yourself very well, lest you forget the things that your eyes saw, and lest these things depart from your heart, all the days of your life, and you shall make them known to your children and to your children's children."[1] I did not think I could ever forget a single word. I came from a very secular family and never had a bat mitzvah. But by this point, I was intimately familiar with all the meandering tones of Torah trope, the stepping-down at

---

1   The Bible quote is from Deuteronomy 4:9; my own translation.

the end of "yechere-e-eee" in Gil's nasal voice, becoming more and more self-assured with each repetition. The portion took them over half an hour to recite, from beginning to end.

Gil would do great, and I would tear out my nonexistent hair. Other parents could at least leave their child alone to practice, for the most part. Close the door—the station had good sound insulation, at least. I did not have that option.

On the first few days, my husband Doron would come in and monologue at me instead, but soon enough, the Haisin crisis consumed all his waking hours too, and he barely came home anymore. Alliance Counterintelligence would send a childcare specialist, who was someone's sixteen-year-old and who would spend most of her time sulking in the opposite corner of our apartment from Gil's room. She also had no idea what to do in our kosher kitchen. I was glad I could not see into the kitchen from Gil's doorway. I didn't understand why they would send a sixteen-year-old to care for a thirteen-year-old, and neither did anyone else. Everyone at work was probably trying to get the Haisin not to raze their neighboring planets with nanotechnology.

I did my hardest to grow in weird directions, to attract attention. All I achieved was becoming misshapen.

Then Doron came home with the communications specialist.

"We met in the stairwell. What a coincidence!" He laughed and scratched under his kippah, embarrassed. "They say they were sent by your workplace." He would not say *Intelligence* out loud even at home, and that was probably for the better.

"Yes." The person nodded, grinning at me. "Great to meet you. I've come to help." I could almost feel my leaves perking up. Finally, someone would change me back! At this point, I would even welcome the annoying crease in the middle of my forehead, my too-broad eyebrows. Everything that Doron told me gave me *character* but that I just thought made me look like a middle-aged grouch.

But this person looked human, not one of those shapechanger species who could transform me.

They davka looked Jewish.

"I'm a communications specialist," they said and shook one of my branches.

My sap sank.

Intelligence still couldn't spare a shapechanger who'd carefully mold me back to my previous form. They couldn't spare anyone. Rachmiel Zonenfeld-Merchavi, communications specialist of the convoluted and old-fashioned name, was apparently a linguist on loan from Contact. Still wearing the appropriate uniform too; its navy blue went well with their reddish-brown curls and light brown skin, and its cap provided a convenient head-covering. No one felt motivated to chase first contact while multiple crises were ongoing even within the Alliance, let alone on the periphery. And surely, a communications specialist would at least be able to help me talk to my family, just like one of them helped debrief me after my assignment.

"They wanted to send someone, um, culturally appropriate," Rachmiel said. I couldn't figure out whether they were male or female until I realized that was exactly the point.

"You mean Jewish?" Doron asked.

"Jewish and nonbinary." Rachmiel grinned.

Gil was positively glowing. Doron looked uneasy. For him, even one trans kid was a lot to deal with, and this was a topic where the two of us frequently clashed too.

I'm a cis woman though, I wanted to say, but I was still a houseplant.

Doron could not stop pestering Rachmiel as they were setting up. "Rachmiel is a male name, isn't it . . .?" he asked.

Gil grimaced. "But Tati, I'm having a *bar* mitzvah, and I'm not a boy either." Said with the intonations, *C'mon, Tati, at least try to make an effort.* After two weeks of listening to Gil's Torah portion, I was even more attuned to nuances in their voice.

"Oh, that's interesting." Rachmiel perked up. "So why are you having a bar mitzvah? I'm curious." I noticed the very clear attempt to distract from the conflict starting to simmer between Doron and Gil. I knew little about Contact, but surely, it could not be all that different from Intelligence, except we never wore uniforms.

"Uh, I dunno, I'm not a fan of the gender-neutral options? B'nei mitzvah sounds weird?" Gil said. "One of my aunts said that the Reform people in her neighborhood call it zera mitzvah, but that's . . . I think that's inappropriate for me at least. I mean sure, *zera* means 'seed,' but it also means 'semen.' That's even more male-gendered than *bar* mitzvah."

Rachmiel grinned. "Well, surely not only men can produce semen."

I thought Doron would explode at this abrupt segue into genital detail, but instead, he laughed. "I did not expect a Torah discussion! Well, you know what the Mishnah says . . ."

I let him ramble on about Mishnaic and Talmudic gender and sex, explaining passages to Rachmiel that I was sure the communications specialist knew inside and out, like I knew Gil's Torah portion. Rachmiel took it all in stride, which was great, seeing that I still had no way to talk.

"Wow, so you're like, a telepath?" Gil stared at Rachmiel in undisguised admiration.

They grinned at the antiquated term. There was something catlike in their demeanor. "I can perceive people's minds, so to say. It's one tool in my Contact toolbox."

"Can I stay to watch?"

"If you want to talk to your mom, you'll have to stick around," Rachmiel said nonchalantly. Gil's head swiveled as they noticed what I long since had: Doron had wandered out of the room. I tried not to feel slighted.

Rachmiel looked at me, keeping me in sharp focus—and I would have shivered if I could at their sudden intensity—and then away into the distance. "So, what would you like to tell your offspring?"

So many things to say. I had no idea where to start.

They keep on mispronouncing "kol tuv" as "kol tov" in the sixth aliya, I thought at them.

"I'm sorry. I'm not good at numbers," Rachmiel smiled back at me with apology in their glimmering eyes. "But I'll try." They turned around. "So Gil, about your Torah portion . . ."

Rachmiel stalked through the apartment after dragging me to the living room. "While your husband is away at work, I can make the two of you food. A stir-fry perhaps?"

That sounded good. I never really considered issues of yichud with nonbinary people before. Would I be allowed to stay at home with this unrelated adult of . . . did this count as the opposite gender? Gil was my own kid, but this was a new situation. And speaking of seeds, what does the Talmud say about sentient houseplants anyway? I was sure there had to be something.

Yichud would not even be an issue for secular people then . . . would it?

That sounds good, I thought at Rachmiel. Surely this was one step up from leaving Gil alone with that girl, even if all they did was sulk. And at this rate, I would remain a houseplant until Haisin nuked its rivals from orbit. *G-d forbid,* I added to myself.

"Are you staying, like, overnight?" Gil asked, sitting down on the sofa.

"I'm staying for as long as you need me," Rachmiel said but stopped mid-stride. "Oh! I forgot. I need to check in. My hours are being tallied as in-home care, and they have a separate system for that." They reached into their pocket and pulled out a boxy, dated-looking communicator. They pressed buttons in a long, complicated string. "Do you know your code numbers?"

Which code numbers? I was perplexed, and Gil likewise.

"For the type of activity, this says." They frowned at the little box.

Gil shrugged. "What does it have?"

"Things like '056 - indoor/outdoor recreational activity' . . .?" Rachmiel pressed more buttons. I thought that even if I knew the appropriate code numbers, I probably could not get them across.

"What does *outdoor* even mean, a spacewalk . . .? I'm sorry. They must've told me at some point what to put in, but I forgot," Rachmiel said.

This would prove to be an ongoing theme.

"This is tasty!" Gil exclaimed, slurping up noodles, and I was happy they didn't try to compare Rachmiel's food to mine. Not that Rachmiel did anything to even attempt to upstage me. They made easy comfort food with Middle Eastern spices and the occasional Asian ingredient. It looked like their own home cooking, and it probably was. Their thoughts were closed to me, even after days of talking . . . and they often missed when I was addressing them. They were easily distracted by their surroundings, their own thoughts, whatever else struck their fancy.

Rachmiel sat and began to munch. "Your mom tells me you've been practicing your Torah portion a lot. Care to share at some point? I do believe she has even more comments on it, and I wasn't sure I got it all across. Maybe you could recite it for us and then she could stop us whenever she had something to say?"

I've been putting this off, and Rachmiel had to know that. Were they meddlesome? I hoped they weren't meddlesome. I was stuck with them for the foreseeable future.

Doron sat down heavily at the dining room table, glanced at the leftovers and then at Rachmiel.

"I need a Talmud chavruta," he said in a voice that came across more like, *I am extremely stressed.*

Rachmiel blinked, and the way their eyes darted around made me wonder if they were searching for an escape route. Alas, my pot was blocking their way to the exit.

". . . thank you. I appreciate that you thought of me," Rachmiel said. Was their voice trembling? "But I, I don't know if I would be an appropriate study partner for you."

Gil looked at me across the table—me, the houseplant—and grimaced. Then they looked back at the last piece of eggplant on their plate.

I was so stunned that somebody who wasn't Rachmiel looked at me that I didn't even understand at first what Gil was trying to get across to me. They had to look back up from the eggplant and make another face.

My thoughts rushed forward, my plant body not supporting them as well as I would have liked. Was I supposed to interject something? How? I could think at Rachmiel, but they didn't look like they were paying any attention to me. And what did Gil have on their mind?

Oh. If Doron was all right with studying with Rachmiel, that meant he saw them as a man. Men were supposed to study with men and women with women, if they wanted to study at all. Rachmiel did not look too happy about that.

My roots need to be watered, I thought at Rachmiel as hard as I could.

No reaction.

Gil poked them with their foot under the table.

Rachmiel twitched so hard I was afraid they would upend the remains of dinner altogether.

My roots! Need to be watered! I thought again.

"Uh, Shoshana is saying she needs to be watered, so I'll quickly . . ." They mumbled and jumped up, glad for the interruption.

I hoped the excess water wouldn't be bothersome.

The next day, Gil threw their bag in a corner and proceeded to lift me onto the pallet with heavy sighs. They rolled me back to their room and repeated the maneuver in reverse.

"I want to tell you something before Rachmiel comes back from the grocery store," they said with a stage whisper. "Or before Tati comes home." I had sent Rachmiel away to be out of Doron's way when he comes back from work, and the young linguist seemed to be glad for that.

I couldn't respond with Rachmiel away. But I could listen.

"Look, Mami, we need to do something about Tati. Like . . . I . . ." They sighed. "This is hard to explain, and it is kind of . . . trans stuff."

Which they ordinarily wouldn't bother explaining to their parents. Us. I fought down a wave of sadness, but I also understood. They went on.

"Some nonbinary people like . . . feel happy if people mistake them for the gender that is not what they were assigned at birth. Like if a transmasculine nonbinary person gets called *sir*. They might be cheered up." They paused. "I am cheered up. A bit. If people think I'm a boy. Even though I'm not quite a boy either. But I'm definitely not a girl." They rubbed at their nose. "But . . . some nonbinary people don't like to be mistaken for any binary gender. And I think Rachmiel doesn't either."

I wasn't quite sure I followed. What had Rachmiel's birth assignment been? I didn't know and felt it would be unseemly to ask. They looked the way I'd always imagined a young King David from the Bible: reddish curls, slightly darker skin than mine, a lanky and androgynous look. I read the disputes, and as far as I was concerned, *admoni*, or "reddish," clearly referred to hair color, not ruddy skin. But—

My sap stopped circulating for a moment. Hadn't I just also assumed? King David was certainly assigned male at birth. It was a good thing I had not tried to compliment Rachmiel with this. They probably heard it a lot. Not many Jewish historical figures are described as having had red hair, even tentatively. And the comparison probably hurt them every single time.

"Mom, are you even paying attention?"

Gil was grumpy. "*I was saying,* we have to get Tati to stop. I asked Dov to ask his Tati to call and say that he's looking for a chavruta. And he did! He called Tati at work! But Tati didn't seem interested in studying with Dov's Tati at all! He . . ." Gil took a deep breath. They were hurting. I was hurting just seeing that. "I think Tati wants to be *inclusive,* and that's why he's been pestering Rachmiel with this whole study thing. But it just makes Rachmiel upset and . . . and intimidated. I tried to tell him this morning after he pestered them some more, but he just brushed me off! Mami . . ."

They looked at me with pleading eyes.

They were finally talking to me, but I couldn't be happy about this. They talked to me because they were upset with their Tati. My husband.

"Hellooo, is anybody home? Where is my family?" Doron bellowed from the doorway.

Gil cast an apologetic glance at me and went out to hug him.

What could I do? Aggressively gendering Rachmiel female wouldn't balance out the situation. It would probably cause double the amount of hurt instead. I was having second thoughts about having sent them to the grocery store even. Was that a feminine activity? But they did seem to be grateful for that . . . only to get away from Doron. Dear Doron. Dear, aggressively clueless Doron. My beloved husband.

I felt resentful of him all of a sudden. Yes, we were both busy with work. But I would always take the time to read the parent guides and gender articles that Gil gave me, even if I was perplexed how most of it would apply in an observant Jewish household. I even fought with Doron when he wanted to take Gil out of the public school in this station wing and make them go to the tiny Jewish school on the far end of Line C. *You don't realize how big this station is?* I had yelled at him. But my argument that had won him over was, *Do you* really *trust the Olimpianer Chasidim to run a school properly?*

I personally thought the Olimpianer Chasidim were fine and among the less unusual offshoots of Chabad Lubavitch, if the most recent. I had been to their big synagogue on Mars, Mons Olympus, and thought it was delightful. So I still felt bad I had said that. But it worked on my stubborn husband, who thought Chasidim were not quite respectable, Lubavitchers among them even less so, and Olimpianer Chasidim—oyyyy, let's not get into that. As he would say, we are not *that* kind of Orthodox.

I had been so preoccupied with my thoughts that I hadn't even realized at first that Doron had come into Gil's room and crouched down in front of me.

"Beloved? I think we need to talk."

Was Gil already off to their fencing practice? And when was Rachmiel coming back?

"I know you can't answer me," Doron said, pained. "And I feel like I should've been spending more time talking to you even when you can't answer." He anxiously smoothed down his beard. "I'm sorry about that."

He paused for so long that I thought he wouldn't say anything else. But then he rubbed his face slowly, determinedly, as if to gain time, took a deep breath, and sighed. "I'm not sure what I'm doing wrong. I want to be welcoming to Rachmiel. But every time I want to ask him, I mean her, I mean them . . . not this again. Every time I ask them to do something with me, they seem more afraid of me. I thought maybe studying would be less intimidating. I had that conversation with them about Tractate Androginos in the Mishnah the first day, and they seemed to welcome it. But now they're just avoiding me." He paused again. He looked like he was about to cry. *Entreat and beg,* I thought to myself. "And even you seem to be helping them avoid me. I don't know what I'm doing wrong."

I couldn't say anything. I wished I could tell him to listen to his own child. I wished I could tell him that he should make an effort, not just for Rachmiel's sake but also for Gil's. I wished he read those books. He read secular literature otherwise just fine. He was in Counterintelligence! And he'd read up on what the Talmud said on gender, if his conversation with Rachmiel was any indication. But could he read a single modern text? Gil was trying so hard to talk to him.

I tried to push all my energies into growing. What else could I do for now but grow? Asymmetrical, askew, but my vitality had to go somewhere. I wished I could caress Doron's cheek and tell him, *It will be all right if you just take a moment to listen to your own family.*

"I'm sure Rachmiel has had a lot of bad experiences with religious people, but *I'm not that person!*" Doron raised his voice. He stifled a sob.

I wanted so badly to reach out to him, to help him. To explain to him that even if he wasn't that person, Rachmiel looked at him and saw a generic Orthodox guy with a generic curly beard, a black kippah, and a white shirt. He did not even tuck his tzitzit into his pants. Every time Rachmiel looked at him, they were reminded of all their former experiences with people like him. It wasn't Doron's fault. But it was something he needed to take into consideration, and he wouldn't, he couldn't, unless I spelled it out to him.

Plants could move, if only so slowly. I tensed up in my whole body, tried to grow in his direction. Just a little bit . . .

The pot overbalanced, and I swung wildly in the air, falling over.

Rachmiel dropped their mesh grocery bags, fresh fruit tumbling out, and I had a random incongruous thought that none of this would have happened if they had just made food using the fabricator.

Doron was kneeling on the floor, trying to hold my pot together. Soil clumps rolled out from gashes in the pottery. I was sure the pot had split clean in half, but I couldn't quite see it. I could only see with my leaves, not with my roots.

"Come and help me!" he yelled at Rachmiel. "She fell over!"

Rachmiel froze, a deer-in-the-headlights moment.

"It wasn't me, all right?" Doron shouted. "The pot just toppled! Quick, get a bigger pot and some soil. We'll need to replant her ASAP!"

I could almost feel how he shoved his emotions down inside himself as his counterintelligence officer habits took over. I seldom if ever saw him like that. Decisive action.

Rachmiel turned to the fabber slowly, as if in a daze.

Doron caught their gaze. "The fabber opening is only half a meter in diameter. This needs at least 60 cm. Go out to the shared one in the corridor. Go!"

Rachmiel shuddered and broke into a run.

"I'm putting her in," Doron said. "Hold the bowl."

The two of them patted down the new soil. Their hands inadvertently touched. Rachmiel twitched but kept on working.

"This . . . this needs to be reported," Rachmiel said on a shaky voice.

"It wasn't me. I'm sorry. It wasn't me," Doron repeated, shock creeping in again now that he'd successfully dealt with the emergency situation. "The pot just toppled over."

"That's not what I'm saying!" Rachmiel grabbed him by the shoulders, smearing him with dirt. "Can you listen for once!"

This time, Doron twitched. I also would have if I could, but then I realized that Rachmiel probably did not observe shomer negia, the prohibition of touch between the opposite sexes. How would they observe it anyway? They couldn't just go around not touching anybody.

"Yes, go on," Doron said. I couldn't make sense of their tone of voice. For all the practice I've had in distinguishing subtleties recently, their intonation was entirely flat.

"It needs to be reported because then they will hurry up and get her a shapechanger!" Rachmiel let go of him as they realized they were squeezing into his arms, but they kept on yelling. "What if I hadn't come home just in time? She could have died!"

I could last for quite a while without major dehydration—I was a Mediterranean plant—but I didn't share that thought with Rachmiel. They had a point.

Doron slowly nodded. "You have a point." He chuckled, unexpectedly but with relief as far as I could tell. "We have a *small* child. Certainly it is dangerous to have a huge plant . . ."

"Bar mitzvah age is not a small child," Rachmiel protested, though with a grin.

"Are you talking about me? I'm back. Class was cancelled because Shawna needed to take her dog to the vet . . ." Gil was standing in the doorway.

"Shawna has a dog? On a space station?" Doron sounded as random as I felt.

"The more important question: why is there a vet on station?" Rachmiel laughed.

"What happened here?" Gil's eyes opened wide as he took in the carnage, soil all over the floor. It did not reabsorb like ordinary stains. The people who designed the station must have thought of planting accidents.

By dinnertime, we were all cleaned up. Doron and Rachmiel spoke to my boss, who spoke to yet more people. There was little else to do. We only needed to put our emotions in order.

"I'm sorry. I was trying to reach out. I didn't realize it was intimidating," Doron said.

"Tati, I was trying to explain." Gil sounded exasperated as usual.

"I know. I'm sorry. I should have listened." He rubbed his face again. Was he developing a new nervous tic?

"You were trying to include me but as a man," Rachmiel said quietly.

"Well, it's . . . hard to include someone in Jewish practice otherwise, especially . . . also seeing I'm a man." Another rub. "And besides."

"That's part of the problem, yes," Rachmiel said.

They were taking this as well as they could, given the circumstances. Whereas I had dramatically broken my pot. And the situation wasn't even about me. I had to remind myself not everything was about me, which was hard in a household where I sometimes felt neglected anyway. It was a defense mechanism.

While I thought that through, the others had already moved on.

"You know what? We can all study Talmud together," Gil said. "In a mixed group."

Did Doron just suppress a gasp? "That's the first time you're showing any interest in the Gemara," he said.

He was right.

"Well, Rachmiel made it sound interesting," Gil nodded. "Tractate Androginos? Nobody told me about that in bar mitzvah prep. But you seemed to know about it." Emphasis on *you* with just a trifle of resentment.

"That's in the Mishnah. It's a tractate that doesn't have a Gemara, per se," Doron said, in his usual lecturing voice, but Rachmiel nodded merrily along.

"Shoshi dear? I'll have a word with his tutor," Doron said, turning to my pot standing at the head of the table. "But for now, we can learn this together. I thought . . . previously . . . that maybe it would be improper for me to encourage, if that's even the right word. I thought maybe they'd grow out of this . . . this interest, but—"

Rachmiel raised a hand. "A moment. I'm getting a call."

We all stared at them as they mumbled yeses and nos, staring into the distance as their interface served up the image of their conversation partner, unseen to us. They finally disconnected. "I'm getting recalled," they said.

Doron frowned. "Another emergency situation? Carryover from Haisin? How are we going to cope without you?"

"No, they're sending the shapechanger tomorrow morning," Rachmiel grinned at me.

Gil looked at Doron and then at me. "But can we still study this evening?"

Doron slapped the table and laughed. "That's what I like to hear!"

Gil whooped, and I had to struggle not to tilt over my new, larger pot. The tension eased.

"But can you . . . can you come over maybe sometime later too? To visit? I really liked talking to you," Gil said to Rachmiel, and I wondered what conversations they had had that I had not been privy to. About gender, certainly, but maybe about other topics as well.

Gil always felt lonely to me, and I could not have more children. I could not provide them with the usual many-kids Orthodox household. But this time, they seemed to have found . . . friendship? Mentorship? I would not take it away from them.

Please do, I thought at Rachmiel with all my strength, and this time they noticed me without anyone else reminding them that I might be trying to speak. They turned toward me, their eyes gleaming. "I would be glad," they said, and the gleam I saw in their eyes when they had arrived was finally back.

I was looking forward to my usual shape, my usual computer interface, my usual everything. But nothing else would quite remain the same. I'd have to educate Doron myself, if his own parents hadn't, if living out here on station hadn't, if working for Alliance Counterintelligence hadn't. Maybe the stereotype was true after all—was Intelligence a more open-minded environment? I knew better than to start an intra-services rivalry with him.

Tell my husband that he should read the books on my nightstand, I told

Rachmiel. *He might learn a thing or two not quite covered by the Gemara . . . and if he really wants, one day, he might write his own commentary.*

Together with Gil, I thought to myself.

FOLDED INTO TENDRIL
AND LEAF

ILIAR

WE WERE OUT IN THE BACKWATERS IN OUR TEACHER'S ROWBOAT WHEN my beloved told me her true name.

I was rowing at a leisurely pace, enjoying the calm weather, the quiet breeze tracing glyphs on my skin, rustling my short tunic. Plants covered the water in large patches, their leaves angular with sawtooth edges. My beloved reached into the stream, her fingers set against the current, and plucked out a hard, prickly seed. She showed it to me—it was grayish brown with multiple horn-like peaks, about the size of a large nut, if more irregularly shaped.

"Careful, it's sharp." She pointed at the tips of the peaks.

Then she flicked her hand and tossed the seed into my lap. I didn't scramble to catch it— always had slower reflexes than her. I poked at the seed cautiously. Its shape reminded me of an ox, ready to gore.

"My name," she said—and from her tone of voice I knew that this would be her true name, given only to the closest of the close: to lovers, friends, and family. "Sulyom, the seed of the water caltrop in Angwari." Then abruptly, with the kind of segue characteristic of her, she said: "In Hlautara, there's no name for the seed, is there? It's just called a seed, or maybe even a fruit, and the plant is called something like a water nut. In Angwari, it's the same word as the iron caltrops you'd throw in front of the enemy's horses in wartime."

"Ah. Battle spikes." I nodded, feeling painfully monolingual. I wanted to learn Angwari, if only to share a secret language with my beloved; would that be an unsuitable motivation? But we were scrambling to finish our studies with Teacher Mirta, and she barely left us any time to ourselves. Teacher Mirta's approach to magic was purely geometric, an interplay of forces and barriers, no chants or even words. It was fascinating and unique, entirely unlike anything we could learn at the state academies, but we struggled to keep up.

Sulyom fished out another caltrop and tossed it into my lap. I watched the muscles move under her skin as her thick arm whipped back and forth. "Back in Angwarya, we made flour from them. It's great in difficult times, when you can't get much else." She nodded at the expanses of caltrop plants covering the water farther out, their leaves forming a pattern that only resolved from close up, merged into a blanket of green from a distance. "There's always plenty to go around."

I stopped rowing and secured the oars. I ran my fingers along the seeds in my lap, careful not to prick myself. "I'm sure people could use it all up if they put their minds to it."

"Iliar, don't be so defeatist," Sulyom said. I hadn't told her my true name; she simply blurted it out. Now we both knew each other's true names. With magic, sometimes details like that bled through, unplanned, between people who were close. And we were inseparable.

Until the war, that is, but at that point, the war was nothing but a faint murmur in the halls of power, little more than drafts of plans to move units to the border regions.

SULYOM

I stopped cutting my hair to show my grief. Iliar had been taken from me to the front lines so long ago. Would she ever return?

My hair frustrated me. I wanted to rip it all out. Before, I'd shave it off every once in a while. Kept it short the rest of the time too. But then I thought—if Iliar returns somehow, she will be able to see my curls. I wanted to show her this, a part of me she had yet to know. My blonde curls were so different from her glossy black hair, which fell almost straight down.

The army took her and left me here with Teacher Mirta. She insisted that she needed at least one student with her to draw water from the well, to feed the animals. She could draw water from the well and feed the animals just fine. I knew she wanted to keep me because I was the angry one. If soldiers of one army or another showed up, I would fight them. I would fight them, and I would win. Or at least hold them back long enough for us to make a run for it.

Yet I was in the hinterlands, and Iliar was serving in the healer corps, probably seeing action more days than not. The world was unfair, and I didn't know how I could fight the entire world all at once.

I'd wanted to go with Iliar, but Teacher Mirta had held me back. I pushed the anger down inside me. All I did these days was push my anger down. All I did. Push it down and get to work. There was plenty of work still.

The front lines were far, and my training went on uninterrupted. It was only my thoughts that drifted, always. Even now, my hands shook, and I dropped the glass tray. Teacher Mirta's family heirloom, filled with cups of herbal tinctures, her work in progress. I scrambled to pick up the pieces. I cut myself, and the concentrated tinctures scalded my hands. I gritted my teeth. I was bleeding onto Teacher's keepsake rug. My stomach spasmed. How much worse could I make this?

Teacher Mirta found me standing above the ruin of her labors, blood dripping from both of my hands, one palm involuntarily closing over the shards I'd gathered. I expected punishment: she wasn't cruel, but she was cold. I took a step back, almost losing my balance.

She looked me over. I noticed she'd paled. She was very light-skinned, from the northern mountains, but now she seemed even lighter, as if the blood flowing out from me had flown out of her too. Even her hair seemed, all of a sudden, brittle as glass.

"I will not punish you," she said evenly. "I will teach you something else. You need to learn the lesson of stillness and calm. Even when your soul aches, you must know when to remain still, and how to hold still for as long as it takes." She gazed into my eyes. I averted my head, a clumsy attempt at hiding my turmoil. "You will spend a fortnight as a plant—a plant of your choice. This will be your lesson." She paused.

I considered it. She'd mentioned this exercise before. I missed Iliar so much

I could claw off my skin, but there was no way of getting her back. We weren't in any immediate danger ourselves. I might as well learn something in the meanwhile. I nodded.

"Most of my previous students who needed this exercise chose a tree." Teacher Mirta paused again. "The ritual involves swallowing the plant's seed."

She did not know my true name. But I would reveal it to her, just for this.

Pain came easy to me.

ILIAR

When I saw the stray guinea pig running to hide under a rotting pile of wood, I knew all was lost. Teacher Mirta had always kept the guinea pigs in a large shed, carefully under lock and key.

To find my way back to Teacher Mirta's house, to my beloved Sulyom, I had wandered through a landscape of lack and deprivation; what the war had not destroyed, the marauding armies had taken for food. Most of the guinea pigs had probably warmed errant soldiers' stomachs.

The closest household was Aunt Karisa's. When she heard me approach, she came to the fence and leaned against it, her body trembling. "I saw the soldiers," she muttered. "They came for the mage and took her. Poor Mirta," she said in such a tone as to brook no confusion about the fate of my teacher.

My body was beginning to take on Aunt Karisa's trembling in sympathetic resonance. "What happened to her student?" I asked.

"Oh, that youngster? About your age? A boy or a girl? I could never figure it out."

"A girl," I told her as firmly as I could manage. Sulyom was somewhere in between, but her body was her own business, not a village auntie's—and she'd always considered herself a girl, grew up as a girl, lived as a girl.

"All right then," she grumbled, "no need to take offense. My eyes are not what they used to be."

I wanted to shake her; some of Sulyom's vehemence that had rubbed off on me. "Yes, but—where is she?"

She shook her head, her blue-printed headscarf slipping. "I don't know. I hadn't seen her in weeks when the soldiers came. I was wondering where she'd gone . . . some of the youngsters from the village ran away to join the army, so I figured . . ." She shook her head again and brushed a thin brown strand of hair that'd escaped from under the scarf behind her ear with unsteady fingers. "That's all I know, my dear."

I'd held myself together through all the battles, through the assault on the ramparts of Samur, but now I struggled not to drop to my knees. I'd come all this way for Sulyom, my boots turning to rags, walked across endless lands for Sulyom—all for nothing?

SULYOM

Teacher Mirta would make me swallow the caltrop, I knew. I craved it. I craved it like I craved the pain that stabbed at me every time I moved my fingers. I wanted to turn against the whole world. I could not, so I turned against myself. The pain could take the possibility of thought away.

Teacher Mirta cleaned and treated my wounds and chemical burns after I'd dropped her glass tray. She bandaged everything carefully. She applied gentle wisps of magic, belying her hard nature.

"I can't heal your hands faster," she said, turning her small pale head to the side like a bird. "Your body struggles against it. You'll have to wait until after your shapechange."

I'd wanted to run away. This was the next best thing.

I dreamt about the ritual the night before the date we had set. The caltrop going down my throat. It felt as if it were one of the iron caltrops laid out to delay marching armies. A weapon. It tore up my mouth, my throat, and I could feel it slicing through my innards. I was splitting open with a nonsensically large wound in keeping with the logic of the dream. I reached into it and turned myself inside out. My damaged hands grabbed my damaged flesh and twisted until what had been inside was on the outside, and what had been hidden inside me all along was a shining gleaming crystal, glowing with sunlight—

I woke with a startle. My chest hurt. Teacher Mirta was sitting at the foot of my bed.

"I had some seeds saved from last year. I made them into a powder," she said and then quietly added: "Not everything needs to be violent, you know."

I knew. I'd come all the way from Angwarya to study with someone who wasn't part of the great academies. Those mages with their elaborate ranks, their willingness to go to war, their saber-rattling—it disgusted me, and I feared it. Teacher Mirta lived out here to avoid people but also to avoid fighting.

I didn't want to fight because I knew I would be good at it.

ILIAR

I wandered around the back—the hothouses all destroyed, the plantings ripped out or eaten by wild animals once the protective enchantments had faded. I couldn't feel anyone's presence, only an odd vibration; maybe the aftershocks of a fight? Sulyom would have fought if she'd been taken by force. Of that, I was certain.

I tried to expand my senses. Everything ought to have been clear, now that the battles had subsided, but I still couldn't get an impression of either Sulyom or Teacher Mirta. I would have felt their passing through our bonds, death reverberated stronger and farther than almost anything, so they had to be alive. I knew little beyond that, and I suspected only because Mirta had warded herself well from our stray thoughts. Where were they? What had happened? Our neighbor had insisted that Sulyom had vanished long before Teacher Mirta was taken. Where could she have gone? Would she have left of her own accord? I hoped desperately that she hadn't run away to find me while I was already on my way back.

In Sanabrou, there was a prison for mages, I knew, warded so tight that not the faintest impression of magic could escape. If Teacher Mirta had been taken there, that would explain why I could not find a trace of her. But what of Sulyom? Some imprint of her lingered still, even if it slipped further away from my attention the more I tried to focus on it. Yet I could not find where she had gone—it was as if she had vanished, dissolved in the heavy, late-summer air.

I walked through Teacher Mirta's small domain. The lake beyond the plant beds was entirely overgrown with water caltrops. It was little more than a pond, really—not even an oxbow lake, maybe a remainder of one. Here, on the edge of the wetlands, it was hard to tell how everything had formed.

Yet I was sure the caltrops had not been there when I had left; they could be found all over the backwaters but not in our teacher's own backyard. Despite all Teacher Mirta's misgivings about symbolism and words, I still felt a tinge of inspiration. I could make use of a caltrop to lead me to Sulyom. I had certainly acquired more skill with location spells while I'd been running from one battle to another, desperately searching for wounded people to heal. It wasn't the abstract interplay of forces Teacher Mirta had taught me—the battle-learned magic had a solidity to it, symbols like little chunks of power. A sulyom could take me to Sulyom. Even if not instantaneously, I didn't have enough raw power for that, but I could always just walk once I had an idea where to go.

I took off my trousers but put my boots back on—stepping onto a caltrop with bare feet would be most unwelcome. I pulled the hem of my tunic between my legs and tied it to my belt. I wobbled closer to the lake, unsteady on uneven ground. I waded into the water—

An odd pressure and then a sharp pain. It took me a moment to realize what had happened, then I swore. The sole of my right boot had split open, the water and the walking and the odd caltrop embedded in the muck altogether proving too much for it.

I hopped backward on one leg, lost my balance, and slipped, falling with a loud *splosh*. Another caltrop wedged itself in my cheek. I grimaced, grabbed it, and shoved it into the side pouch clipped to my belt, but one of its tips broke off and lodged in the flesh of my palm.

This, at least, was one trial I could overcome. I stood, favoring my left leg, and closed my eyes to better direct my magic. There was an odd moment of hesitation as if the universe itself was holding its breath. Then the fragment popped out, and the skin pulled together with that uneasy and all-too-familiar sensation of flesh moving as if under its own will.

I opened my eyes and walked back to the grass where I could sit, hoping nothing would sting or bite me. I could heal my foot, but I'd need to find a new pair of boots—inanimate objects were much harder for me to fix. At least I'd had enough presence of mind to preserve a caltrop.

The two healings were small but finicky and left me hungry and lightheaded. I'd left my backpack in the remains of my former room. I wondered if I should go back inside. Someone had ransacked the house while I was out on the front lines—had they been looking for something valuable or just some dried fruit and meat stashed away somewhere? I hadn't left much for people to find, and even the supplies in my backpack were beginning to dwindle.

I couldn't take the time to eat. I had to know. I took the caltrop out of my pouch, held it delicately between three fingers, and focused on the sensation at my fingertips; the hardness and potential for violence coiled within the seed. Closed my eyes again, tracing lines of influence and belonging.

My eyes popped open of their own accord. The trail led nowhere. It was as if Sulyom were right there, standing in front of me. What was I doing wrong?

I threw the caltrop back into the lake, my eyes smarting with sudden tears.

SULYOM

This, then, was the punishment: I couldn't remember the change. The change I'd craved. The chance to get out of my flesh. Just one faint memory of Teacher Mirta peeling apart the muscles of my limbs, thread by thread. Nothing else was left.

Just the water, just my width and breadth, weighing down and floating. Held up.

I wasn't motionless; I wasn't paralyzed. But movement was slow. Sensation was slow. Thinking was slow. Above me was sunlight on air, below me water, my bulk separating it from the sun. Fish scurried out from underneath me, escaping the lack of brightness.

One day, I thought, *Trees can support humanlike thought much better*, Teacher Mirta had said.

Another day, I thought, *I should have chosen a tree.*

Another day, *Then again, we both enjoy a challenge*, she had said, faintly amused.

Another day, *How much time yet to a fortnight?*

Then I didn't think about time anymore. It was hard to produce thought. I didn't force it. I grew, expanded. I would grow seed. Cover the pond, the struggling fish; I hadn't considered the fish, but it wasn't as if I could expand any slower. There was only the pattern of sunlight on leaves, rain and darkness on leaves, my weight held up by the water. Roots were hard to figure out, but I knew from what remained of my human memories that my leafy rosettes would eventually detach from the roots remaining in the soil, and I would swim on the surface. It felt strange now. But it wouldn't happen in a fortnight.

I gradually eased into the days and into my new existence. The pain not so acute, the pain in the soul. The lesson being learned deep in the body.

ILIAR

I shook out the bedspread and fell on top of it. I had to find Sulyom, but first, I had to get some rest, and the next day I could rethink my approach. The war had taught me how to fall asleep anytime, anyplace.

I woke from a dreamless night with a shock, as if something had pricked me. I searched around, patted down my bed. Something dropped to the floor. The water caltrop I'd picked from the lake? Hadn't I thrown it back into the water?

I gasped, suddenly reminded of the changing ritual Teacher Mirta had always brought up whenever one of us apprentices had grown sloppy and unguarded in our haste, our eagerness to learn. *I will turn you into a tree yet. I learned much from my time as a tree at your age.* We joked behind her back that it'd turned her heartless, and we were sure she'd heard, but she never showed any sign that she did. She was such a grouch, but she wasn't mean-spirited.

Yet Sulyom had not been turned into a tree, had they? A blanket of water caltrops rather.

All the stray magical impressions I'd discarded earlier fit into place. This made sense, the kind of symbolic sense I'd learned to handle after I'd left here. I'd only ever felt lonely, out of my depth, but maybe I'd acquired some independence too.

After the wave of relief, a sudden fear took my breath—the change so sharp that I almost choked on the air.

The water caltrop was an annual plant, not a perennial. And the season was ending.

SULYOM

Large animals arrived. People arrived. I couldn't distinguish between the two with my new senses, and my human magic was somewhere out of reach. All my anger was someplace else. My fast, snappy thoughts, someplace else. The torrent of magic at *my* control, someplace else.

I didn't understand speech. I couldn't follow rapid movements. My teacher thought desperately at me, but I couldn't understand her words or even her intentions. It all happened too fast.

The plants in the beds exuded warning chemicals that should have helped me prepare, but I couldn't. I understood the signal, but I wasn't able to escape, and neither were they. The hothouses were broken open, the plants within becoming accessible to my plant-senses—then destroyed in rapid succession. Decay floated in the air, spoiling even the sunlight.

Were these enemy soldiers? What were they hoping to find?

I was helpless with no access to my one talent, the one that had ensured I would be left here: to fight, to defend the one person who had made me helpless and unable to protect her.

I spent days piecing together my impressions, thought forced through my stems like sap, and finally, I understood. These hadn't been enemy soldiers. They couldn't have reached us so fast. These soldiers had been of this country. Soldiers of Hlautar. And my teacher had trusted them.

ILIAR

I had to turn Sulyom back into her human shape. I knew nothing about spells of change, but I knew about healing: you couldn't make a wound close while holding it open. I knew about general principles before coming here, and then from Teacher Mirta I had learned about processes, and in the war, I had learned about symbols. I could cobble something together.

I gathered a bundle of objects that looked at least somewhat valuable—a carving of northern animals, a spice holder, a knife with a bone handle—and gave them to Aunt Karisa to trade for a pair of sturdy boots, the ones the fisherfolk used. While she was making her usual weekly journey to the market, I tied back my hair and set to encircle the small lake with rope. It would have a dual use: both magical and practical. I found a set of pegs in one of the storage rooms but no hammer: it was a struggle to find purchase in the soil, just far enough from the water that the ground was less slippery, but not as far as to use up too much rope.

I had an idea, but I wasn't sure I could carry it out. Once the lopsided circle was complete, I needed to get some of the rope over the water, to draw out chords as long as I could make. I tried tying one end of the rope to a stone and throwing, but my attempts didn't even make it halfway across. I wished I had a crossbow. I'd need to swim again just to get the rope exactly where I wanted it. I imagined a giant star shape.

Once I had my boots, I waded. I thought about putting on heavy clothing to protect myself, but I was worried about drowning, even in shallow water. Yet this time around, it was as if the angry, biting seeds had swum out of my way. I could feel that my theory was correct—and I could feel Sulyom gathering her mind together from each tiny leaf floating on the surface, slowly coming together in an attempt to aid me. How could I have missed it the first time?

This time I knew what I was doing, and I would not give up. I would get her back.

Once I had the cords of rope across the lake, forming a star, I began to gather the plants in the center. Teacher Mirta would have disapproved of such crude symbolism, but in war, there was little time for abstract elegance. A star shape focused energy well, bringing a hundred suns to mind. It would do.

The water caltrop had initially been rooted in the wet soil, but as the season passed, at least some of the plants detached and floated, and the remaining roots were light and fragile. Yet the masses of plants were heavy, unwieldy, and I could not quite figure out how to use my magic to aid this process. I slogged, wet to the bone, occasionally wracked by sobs, but I routed all my terror, my helplessness, my sense of incompetence, back into my magic—just like my love, my terrified shaking fear of losing the one I loved after I'd walked across a continent and found her.

The fear subsided as I worked, turned into a whole-body thrum that kept me warm and allowed me to focus on Sulyom: her shape, her askew apologetic smile that I loved, her hair she liked to shave to the scalp and always promised to grow out but never did, her broad, wide shoulders, her jaw that made people think she was a boy, her short thick arms and legs, everything everything, the hair on the smooth curve of her belly, the roundness and angles, the beauty, the beauty, my own crushing need.

A body, slowly coalescing, my fingers scrambling to tie limbs together lest they fray again, lest they disintegrate.

SULYOM

There was a sense of being gathered, pulled this way and that. Perturbing yet familiar. A large animal: a person. A person I knew was yanking me around, piling leaf upon leaf until I was blocking the sunlight from myself.

It was purposeful, like the warnings of dying plants in the hothouse. It was important. I strained to pull myself together, body and mind.

My shape: limbs forming. Stems tied together, unnatural yet remembered. I had been like this before. Once.

Iliar brought me back, but I couldn't speak. My body felt soggy and ponderous once out of the water. My mouth couldn't make the right motions. I was beginning to turn human, but my body didn't know what to circulate. What was blood? I was losing my green.

I coughed, all of a sudden desperate for air.

ILIAR

Her body was heavy, and I had to overstrain my magic to convince it to keep asserting its shape. The water was too tempting, returning into plantness was too tempting. I dragged us out: Sulyom couldn't quite walk but could put a leg forward and then another, and I pushed, shoved, pulled. Coughs wracked her, and I feared she would fall apart.

She sat by the water in the blanket I'd wrapped around her, gazing at the lake, breathing very slowly and existing very slowly, and I knew that some of her was still plant.

I could try to adjust her nervous system; I'd treated so many soldiers with head injuries, back injuries, neck injuries. Usually, all I could do was help the body heal itself. You couldn't restore an original state. In those days, I'd reminded myself of my teacher's words: change was how the mind worked. The outcome was always different. You never stepped into the same waters twice.

I would wait it out.

SULYOM

Why had Teacher Mirta trusted the soldiers? Had she? What had happened? Now that I was back on dry land, on my two feet, all my anger came flooding back. My lesson had not gone as planned. Had I learned anything?

She was always an advocate of peace. Had she sabotaged her own defense? I hadn't thought we'd be attacked either. I was naive. But she was so much more experienced! I didn't even have words for my helpless fury.

I had to find her. I had to ask her why.

I couldn't feel her magic. But I could feel her, plant to plant to plant.

ILIAR

"The anger helps," Sulyom finally said, pausing between each word—not waiting but hesitating. She bit her lip, her fingers scrabbling in the mud. I felt her words like caltrops, sharp and uncomfortable to hold. "I like being plant. I also like being human. I need to be . . ." she stopped for so long I thought she wouldn't finish the sentence. "Both. I must."

"I'm here," I said and stopped myself from asking, *How can I help?* Sulyom wouldn't know—and who could? People didn't stay plants for many months on end, struggling to find their way back. The exercise was never supposed to last this long. "I'll try to help as best as I can," I finally said.

I also stopped myself from saying, *Why do you need to be both?* I knew one could never return to a previous state entirely. The mind grew, like a plant—and this was good. Attempts at fixing people never came out right, and attempts at fixing people's minds even more so. I've seen this enough in my healing work.

But there was something here I still didn't understand, some kind of help I could offer if only I could figure out what Sulyom needed.

"Please ask," she said. "Ask."

What should I ask? She needed to be both—why, beyond the fact that she was already both and there was no reverting that?

"Where is Teacher Mirta?" I asked, and Sulyom sagged. Some kind of tension I hadn't even noticed was suddenly leaving her body. Was this the right question?

"I sense her," she said. "Through plants."

SULYOM

Iliar came back for me. Iliar fought for me. Iliar *was* fighting for me. I turned the thought around in myself, in memories and sense-impressions. It gave me myself.

I had to explain it to her somehow.

Our teacher was imprisoned, and I could feel the magical wards around her basement cell. Nothing could get in and out. Yet I could perceive her. The cell had a narrow, barred window for human sense-impressions. For sunlight. Next to the window grew the roots of a majestic linden tree, some clumps of grass. I could not sense Teacher Mirta seeing the linden tree. Her mind was blocked by the wards. But the linden tree was sensing her. With plant-sight, plant-awareness. Some of it was chemical, I knew. Some maybe magical? I wasn't sure. But it wasn't human magic, animal magic. It hadn't been warded against.

The linden tree could sense her, and the ash tree on the corner could sense the linden tree, and the brush whose name was unknown to me could sense the ash tree, and so on all the way to me.

It was a slow but systematic propagation. Like seed or pollen. Like water seeping into roots. A substance permeating a membrane and then another. When I reached out through the trees, I wasn't sure if I was aware of the now, the near-past, or the long-gone. Teacher Mirta was gaunt in the darkness of her cell, even thinner than usual. A smaller animal instead of a large animal—but with something odd to her. Something plantlike. From her time spent as a tree? Was she still tree in some way? Like the plants in the hothouse, she was experiencing distress.

I grabbed a stick and began to draw diagrams in the mud. Iliar was very close. She wasn't plant, not even a little. Yet somehow that was all right.

ILIAR

Sulyom was drawing with great determination, jabbing the stick into the soggy dirt, yet for all her effort, I couldn't understand. She drew a spiderweb-shape and then something akin to little frog-hops. She was close to tears as each of my guesses missed the mark.

I finally put a hand on top of the shape she had scratched into the earth, turned her head toward me, and looked into her eyes. I didn't need to cast a spell for this—our closeness would make the magic carry, organize itself into abstract processes even Teacher Mirta could appreciate. I nodded, and Sulyom nodded back.

I couldn't assimilate the plantness inside her, within her—my mind would just slide over it. But she focused on human-images, human-senses, converting her impressions into something I could understand, even if with difficulty. She could sense Teacher Mirta through a vast network of plants, the older trees its hubs with an infinite number of spokes connecting them. The network ended in a few clumps of grass across from a basement grating by the roots of a linden tree. The longer I waited, the more detail I saw. Surely a tree could not sense in such visual detail; this had to be some form of extrapolation by Sulyom's mind, or was it? Teacher Mirta stared at each blade of grass with unspeakable longing written on her face, but her thoughts were well-shielded behind the wards, invisible to plant-life.

I contemplated this, the plantness slowing me down. I couldn't reach Teacher Mirta magically. Yet I could reach the linden tree outside the building, and I could use that for a location spell. I didn't have enough raw power to *move* to the target of my spell, but Sulyom could help with that. The two of us could put this together. We used to work well together, and for a moment, fear twinged in me: that was before. Before the war, before our paths diverged and Sulyom turned into a giant mat of water caltrops and I learned all the magic of word-chunks, symbol-chunks that hadn't quite meshed with our previous approach. Yet we were still the same people and still (I squeezed her hand) in love.

SULYOM

This was something I could do. This was something I would do, and right away—

Iliar grabbed my arm. "Don't rush into it. We're doing this together."

I grinned at her. "Together means . . . with me. *I'm* rushing into it. It's my way. I need answers: what went wrong. What happened."

She chuckled. "I thought you were supposed to learn patience from your time as a plant."

"I was very patient. All the impatience gathered up in me, and now, it's free." I made a bursting motion with my hands. Swim, swim little caltrops!

She laughed again and we hugged for the span of a long breath. Then we rolled sideways, folded into tendril and leaf.

      The location spell,

                    the plant-senses,

     the translocation spell,

  the raw power

    hers

and mine

      it all fit together like the teeth of two combs. Like the fingers on two hands intertwined.

My words, her sentences.

We toppled out into an interior courtyard, our backs to a linden tree.

"Hush, there are guards," Iliar whispered. I reached out—through the plants, but also at the same time with my human magic, and the two overlapped —

a structure rising up that encompassed both.

I improvised. Nothing could have foretold this moment. Structure beyond structure.

The prison cell was warded to prevent anything from leaving, not to prevent anything from entering. For that, there were the guards, courtyards within courtyards, iron gates. No one was supposed to get this close.

I grabbed Iliar by the hand and turned. We rolled into the cell, passing through wall and ground and anything else in the way.

ILIAR

I turned around, disoriented. Teacher Mirta was sitting on a grimy cot in one corner, her back straight. Across from her, dust floating in the air glinted in the light of the narrow, barred window-slit at the ceiling.

"Well, you're in. Now how do you propose to get out?" Teacher Mirta's words were bone dry, but there was something unexpected in her facial expression, the way her eyebrows rose. Some kind of warmth perhaps?

"I didn't plan," Sulyom shook her head. "That far."

"I can see that."

Sulyom grimaced. "I'll fight my way out. But Teacher, what happened?"

The two of them glared at each other.

"You could, in principle, fight your way out," Teacher Mirta said. "But it would worsen my political position even further."

"My question! What happened?!" Sulyom was yelling. I winced, took a step back, and bumped into the rough-hewn wall.

"Patience finally ran out," Teacher Mirta said, unfazed. "Allegations were made."

I also felt an urge to yell at her: could she stop with the passive voice? But it would hardly be seemly to shout at my teacher. I didn't understand what was happening. "What kinds of allegations?"

"Several kinds of treason . . . sabotage . . . I believe even espionage, though at some point I must confess I lost track." Her voice sounded more bitter now than dry.

What was going on? Surely these allegations were false; I knew my teacher well enough to know that she owed allegiance to no one besides herself. "Espionage? Sabotage?" I echoed the words, confounded.

"'Holding back resources from the war effort' was how they phrased it," Teacher Mirta responded. "Hiding your fellow student."

"Did you?" Sulyom demanded. The air was becoming thick with magic, as if with humidity.

Teacher Mirta looked away. "Not on purpose. I was expecting my connections from back in the day to serve me for a while yet. I wasn't anticipating soldiers on my doorstep." She took a shaky breath. "I only found out here in prison that Governor Atzin had resigned."

Sulyom hissed in surprise, but I felt ashamed. What did this mean? I had always told myself I was focusing on my studies, that was why I couldn't pay attention to politics. But politics had spattered me in blood and left people dying in my arms. I had been worrying whether Sulyom could understand speech enough to make sense of Teacher Mirta's convoluted sentences, but I couldn't make sense of *anything* while Sulyom was busy nodding. She wasn't even from here . . .?

I realized with a startle that that was exactly the reason. Sulyom understood because she had to—because for a long while, even before the war, her existence turned on knowing the political context and adjusting her plans accordingly. She'd never had the luxury of not paying attention.

SULYOM

I knew it would come to this. Teacher Mirta had never joined the mage guilds. The associations. The organizations for the war effort. In peacetime, it was tolerated, being the odd one out. Like me. In war? I already found out.

She had relinquished a student but kept another. Kept me. Saved me from having to kill. She'd known that Iliar the healer would make it through. Sent Iliar to keep me, but they came and took her away. For who knows what they claimed she plotted. I had to struggle to understand her words, had to reach out with my mind, but this I understood even without her saying anything. Lack of enthusiasm was one thing; *holding back resources from the war effort* was another.

If the soldiers had managed to find me, if I had not been plant, they might have taken me and left her.

Or they might have taken us both.

My voice rose higher and higher. Would that alert the guards? I couldn't remain quiet. "Would you still have done it? If you knew the soldiers were coming?"

She glared back. "Yes. Yes, I think I would."

"You risked my life!" I was trembling. Fear flashed through me that my body might split apart into stem and leaf.

"You don't know the alternative!"

I opened my mouth and then closed it. I knew Teacher Mirta had served the crown of Hlautar in her youth. She never told me the details, but I could imagine them. Still, I didn't have my peace.

I couldn't leave it unsaid. "You abandoned me!" I screamed at her.

She raised a hand, and all around us the cell shifted, changed. She shouted back at me in a way I'd never heard her shout: "I was trying to come back!"

ILIAR

A pattern flashed in the room, just for an instant. Even after it vanished, I could no longer unsee it: it was hidden in every pebble on the floor, every piece of straw, every odd scratch on the forbidding stone walls. It added up to something that filled the space, a third dimension emerging from two, a fourth remerging from three? My mind hurt.

She cleared her throat and began again, calmer this time. "The gate isn't finished yet. I still need to add five more layers to the central sphere to amplify my power sufficiently to bypass the wards. But now that the two of you are here . . ."

Sulyom backed down, and in her face, I noticed that childlike wonder I had not seen for so long, that eagerness to know, to learn more about magic that had driven her to Teacher Mirta. The spirit of free thought that the academies had long since discarded, on all sides of the ever shifting but sharply drawn borders, in favor of a thirst for destruction.

Sulyom reached out with one hand and evoked the gate again with such sudden grace that the realization struck me: this was what her power was suited for, once her anger found a way to be directed. This and not fighting; this and not killing. She stared into the pattern that I could barely behold with a cursory glance. "I . . . see," she muttered.

Teacher Mirta nodded, getting to her feet with some difficulty. "The two of you can assist me. These processes can hold enough power without further amplification already, with three of us."

Something in the back of my head registered that she said *processes* and not *structures*, where I would have certainly called it a *structure*. But I had come to accept that there were many ways to approach magic.

I reached out to the central sphere that was not a sphere, through the entire incomprehensive setup. Maybe if I could think of what I was doing as a healing, that would make it easier. It didn't need to be fixed, just allowed to balance itself. I halted, my fingers up against thin air. "Where do we go now?" I asked. If she couldn't stay in Hlautar, then that had to mean she was going over to the other side, to those who spent their time trying to kill the people I was trying my best to patch up—

"There are more than two sides, and there are more than two places." Teacher Mirta sounded irritated.

Sulyom almost jumped. Anger and fear radiated from her in equal measure. "If you're thinking of Angwarya, Teacher, the Minister-President is just about to declare—"

Teacher Mirta's gaze could have flattened a mountain. "I was *not* thinking of Angwarya. Not every land is embroiled in this conflict yet."

SULYOM

Jumping into the unknown was familiar. I'd declined offers from three academies. I'd come all the way from Angwarya to study with Teacher Mirta. I'd met my beloved here. Iliar had walked across the continent to come back to me. Everything carried a risk, and in many places, we were unwelcome. I didn't want to be a *resource*. I didn't want to be coerced to fight.

I didn't mind running, and I didn't mind danger—as long as I was with my beloved.

I didn't hold my breath through the passage—I stopped doing that when I was plant.

ILIAR

It was weeks before we got close to water again; weeks before we got to a place where we could begin to settle down, at least temporarily. We found three oxbow lakes surrounded by a forest, a forgotten backwater with no villages nearby; the river that had birthed the lakes now flowed farther to the north.

Sulyom waded into the water, laughing, pulling a floating plant with large, cabbage-like leaves away from the surface. Droplets gleamed on it in the early morning sunlight. The plant was attached to another identical-looking plant by a green stalk, and that to another and to another, all floating on the water.

"Water lettuce," Sulyom yelled in delight. "Teacher Mirta said."

"I've never seen anything like that." I wobbled closer, my swimsuit a size too large—just like Sulyom's. We had what we could find. I gestured at the expanse of green. "This one also seems to grow at a frantic pace."

"You can't make—what is it?—flour out of it." Sulyom let the water lettuce drop back into the water and closed her eyes. "It doesn't belong here, but it likes it here. Maybe a bit too much."

Was this a metaphor? Sulyom was not as given to metaphor and symbol as I was. It was probably an impression through the plant-sense. I chuckled. "Too much indeed. One of these days, we'll even be able to afford a new boat."

"One of these days, we'll be able to stop running." She dove under, resurfacing next to me. I ran a hand through the short, stubbly hair on her head—she'd changed her mind about growing it out yet again. I liked the curls, but I also liked this particular sensation.

Sulyom giggled, her voice rising and dropping. I hugged her, and she hugged me back, tilted with me back into the water with a loud splash. I got water into my nose and sputtered, but then it was my turn to dive at her, for us to fall back together again. Her closeness also gave me an impression of her magic, and the field of water lettuce beyond started to glow—not with an emerald sheen but with something invisible to the eye. Threads connected, reached all the way to the horizon. I stopped moving and just floated, soaking in the impression.

Sulyom floated next to me. "I give you this," she said. "Give me something."

What could I give? I opened my mind, seeing symbol interlinked with symbol, our migration and the migration of the water lettuce, our togetherness like two halves of a whole, and even further—because magic didn't only consist of Sulyom's magic and my magic, but many other different kinds besides. Even Teacher Mirta's unfathomable vectors and gradients fit into a united yet manifold whole.

I shivered, the vision vanishing. "Wait a moment, where is she? She was supposed to be back from town by now." The glow of connection—could it have been . . .?

Sulyom prodded the water lettuce and chuckled. "*Someone's* experimenting with new shapes," she said.

I stared for a long moment. "I . . . hope I won't have to change her back too." At least the water lettuce seemed sturdier than the caltrops.

"She has it worked out." Sulyom paused. "I guess."

"That's one way to hide, certainly . . ." Would the wars ever end? Would we ever be able to stop running?

I knitted my fingers together with Sulyom's and watched as the floating mat moved slightly, shuddered as if from the wind, the large upright leaves waving stronger and stronger until I had to avert my gaze from the sight—the intensity of it all, the complexity of it all.

I could learn this. We could learn this together. I looked up to the sky—deep inside myself, I could feel the seed of a new promise take root, begin to grow.

THE THIRD EXTENSION

WE SEEK OUT CHEAP RENTALS; AS LONG AS THE HOUSE HAS A GARDEN, it will suit. The Chasidic mystics say that, to hasten the coming of the Messiah, Jews need to gather the divine sparks scattered across the world. That's the closest parallel we've found, the nearest concept.

We are from a faraway place, near but far, the underside of the world. Do you remember that time from your childhood when with much effort you flipped over a large rock, and bugs were massing underneath? The world flips over and there we are. Not insects exactly but not human either.

We take good care of the rentals—patch the walls, put up new shower curtains, fix that persistent leak in the basement. We want to avoid suspicion. On this side, we never speak in chirps.

Plants grow with their roots into the earth, with their stalks toward the sky, but it is their third extension that concerns us the most.

The third extension grows into the underside of the world where it forms giant caverns if the plants are satisfied, twisty tunnels if they are ailing. We do not live in the caverns or the tunnels; we live on the smooth, warm underside of deserts, and when the rains come and the blooms start, we evacuate with much haste. We grow food in the caverns, our fungal mats needing the room and shelter.

Have you seen what gardens some of these rentals have? There is little in this world that can be as neglected as abandoned artifice. When a garden is set up to be mowed, trimmed, pruned, regularly weeded, and aerated—and I beg you, do not forget about the mole traps—then it does not maintain its equilibrium on its own.

At first, we tried to let our gardens return to their natural state; it does happen with sufficient time. Then the municipality fines started coming in. We ignored the mailings, the warnings tucked under our doors. Then the people brought giant mowers, chewed up vegetation, not letting us have a choice. We were decreasing the value of the neighborhood, they claimed.

So now we mow, trim, prune, weed, and if the mood strikes us, even aerate, ambling across our lawns with our special aerating shoes. We do not let loose our offspring. We smile at the neighbors and put our gardening tools out of sight.

Sometimes, we sneak into recently abandoned lots with our pruning shears, and when we flip the world over and return, we enjoy our bounty. The brash among us ask if it could be easier to simply get rid of humans once and for all, but we are gentle and mild-mannered.

We know these humans will not stay forever.

ON GOOD FRIDAY THE RAVEN WASHES ITS YOUNG

On Good Friday, the raven washes its young,
as this world curses me with frogs and snaketongue;
so this world should tell me face to face,
who have I wronged in my life in this place.

—Hungarian folk song

PLOSH CREAK. THE DOCKS ARE RUSTING APART, THE LITTLE GANGWAYS slowly devoured by all the alien chemicals in the sea. I slip, cuss. I want to be underwater; I want to be treasured. I want to feel like my body does what it was meant to do. Up here, I trundle, out of my element.

I clear my throat—it's always hard to get started—and then I trill to my bathysphere and watch as it pops to the surface and swims closer, its air sacs letting out little puffs. Responding to my call.

It's organic but not sentient; sometimes I wish it were, for then I wouldn't be this alone, this abandoned. The family didn't want a freak, so I came all the way here, to the planetfrontier.

Another pop as the bathysphere opens, and I hop in, start strapping myself into the frame. I take a deep breath. The spinal connectors snake into their slots, and I close my eyes, decouple from my own sensorium.

I'm in the sea; I'm a glowing bubble of magic, and I light up the murky depths as I descend. Not so fast, not so slow—all just an optimization problem of how to gather most of the organic material that craves this influx of magic. On Earth, there are whales, and when they die out in the deepwaters, they sink slowly to the ocean floor, feeding a whole host of marine life. But Earth is low in ambient magic. Things work differently here.

I shine, a beacon, a strength of strengths. Critters tack onto my sphere, grasp me with their mandibles, hug me with their tentacles. I am life, and they hold on fiercely. So little of me to go around. They fight, they jostle each other out of place, they bite and tear and chomp and crunch. They love, they hate.

They look so much like the humans upside, always tearing at me, trying to wound, to hurt. The humans I cannot forgive. The sea life? I'm taking it to its doom.

The pressure holds me tight. I position myself on the ocean floor. I flare my anger around the sphere, detaching the vast, matlike clutter of animal and plant and fungus and whatnot, already compressed into death. A giant shadow passes me by, just for an instant, the memory of a being incomprehensibly larger than my bathysphere. I try to extend my awareness, but the shape is already past; I'm not sure if I just imagined it or if it's actively hiding itself. Or maybe it is indeed just a memory.

We killed all the megafauna. We killed the starfloats, the pecan-whales, hunted the gömböc to extinction and hauled their corpses after our ships, feasted on their meat, sold it off-planet as a delicacy. And then the sea began to die with no giant animals sinking to its depths to feed it any more.

Had this been Earth, everything would've churned upon itself, slowly shriveling up into oblivion with the occasional burst of gas. A silent demise.

Here, the sea turned on us with a ferocity of nightmares, wailing in our minds, its fingers pulling greedily at our thoughts. Mine mine mine. Ceaseless magic rerouted by our actions, turned malignant due to being wrenched out of place. So now we feed the planet. Thus the planet feeds on me: all the power I use to drag organic matter down below, all my effort to mimic a dying starfloat or a gömböc. I resurface, task accomplished, feeling drained and weary. I scramble out into the docks, hoping beyond hope that they wouldn't be there, waiting.

"Hey, the herm. Dude in a skirt!"

I'm wearing wetsuit pants. "Piss off," I mutter. The guy gets in my face, holds firm while my feet slip this way and that. I'm too exhausted even to shove him away. He makes a grab for my shoulders.

On impulse—last-moment, life-or-death impulse—I jump into the water, duck under the piers, swim away from him with the renewing force of anger. "Crazy bitch," he screams after me with more incredulity than violence. I seem to have turned female in his mind.

And I seem to be turning into something else as well, for the water against the bare skin of my face doesn't sting anymore.

I cuss just for good measure as I drag myself out of the sea, well away from him. Down below, I am the life-bringer; if those creatures could worship me, they would. Up here? I'm the guy in the skirt.

It would be easy to blame it on the magic, I think. It confused my hormones, genetics, whatever there is. Except I was born on Earth, and my genes must've been set firmly in place before I came to the frontier as a child. My atypicality became apparent at puberty, which is also when magic tends to manifest, but how much of that was a coincidence, I don't know.

On the ocean floor, I feel a certainty that I am right, just as I was meant to be. But up here, my body is yanking me this way and that. Am I only off-balance because the planet is ailing? Or is that explanation too facile?

I drag myself to the seaside blocks of apartments, stare at the empty expanse of sky and water for long minutes before I turn to my door. I imagine the water rising. Alas, it never reaches this high.

In my home-berth, I undress, wrap myself into layers of blankets. Before I know, I am asleep, and the planet doesn't scream at me; it only drones and drones like a lone electric guitar in some minimalist composition.

> *I came to you: an upstanding young man,*
> *here to pour dew on beautiful women,*
> *because if I don't water them this year,*
> *they won't bloom and flower next year.*

—Hungarian folk rhyme

"Fagtastic, eeeyah!"

And another voice, a drunken baritone:

"Open the fucken door!"

Go away, I think. *Go away.*

I wanted to sleep in—at least on Easter Monday if I didn't get Sunday off. But nature doesn't abide by our festivals, and the sea is ever hungry. I pull my blanket over my head. The dudes outside are thumping on the door.

"You sure it's a woman?"

"You pour the water, and we see!"

"Ooo, boob joke!"

I always, always hated Easter Monday, and that was before these ridiculous right-wing traditionalists decided to bring back the custom of dumping an entire bucketful of cold water on girls. We are not on Earth anymore, but they just have to do this. Go to great lengths to make people miserable.

Will they ever go away?

I wait. Get dressed. They thump and yell. I eat breakfast.

Then they break open the door.

They are surprised, to their credit. They stand there for a moment like a grotesque tableau, the smell of alcohol rising off their skin, strong over the acidic smell of seawater.

I yell, "Now you've gone and got me really angry!" I kick my stool away, push the table into the wall where it vanishes with a loud glop. "*A*, get the hell out of here, *B*, get someone to fix my door!"

One of them whips out the bucket and swings it forward, drenches me completely. Seawater. Caustic, abrasive chemicals.

I smile. Lick my lips. Cross my arms across my soaked torso.

This is very, very much not what they expected.

I raise my right arm to point at them, and outside, the sea rumbles.

They run away.

> *Oh my God, tell me what should I do,*
> *should I run away or should I stop?*
> *If I run, they will chase me still,*
> *If I stay, they will beat me till I drop.*
> —Beás, Hungarian and Romani folk song

I wander the seaside. *That wasn't a prank,* I'm thinking. *They wanted to hurt me, maim me.*

I focus on the magic inside me, the incandescent light. I don't want to return the hurt; I don't want to take revenge. I just want to be left alone.

I pause. Truly? Alone?

I trill, and my bathysphere comes, so fast it had to have been lurking in the shallow water nearby.

Could I give up the land, move into the sea? Would I have to choose sides? Humans or the planet? *The planet, definitely*—I suppress a bitter grimace. But what would that solve?

"The water doesn't sting you either," I tell my sphere. I wonder how it is with the other magical people; I'm always uncomfortable around them. They are all into the same traditionalist nonsense, here on the planetfrontier.

The bathysphere is silent. It doesn't speak. It's an animal.

I pause. An animal. Smaller than the vast megafauna but descended from the same lines.

I smack my lips together and think rapidly, furiously—if I could summon one of the old giants hiding somewhere still, as legend has it—though I never allowed myself this thought before because I was afraid what the *other humans* would do, but I disclaim them, part from them now in order to help them. Life will persist, but it remains to be seen in which shape.

I remember the shadows of the sea. And I remember the soft droning sound. I start to hum, the melody resonating between my teeth.

I would not summon the giant, gentle-seeming beings to satisfy my curiosity, nor to lead hunters to them. I would not call out to beings, who might be the very last of their kind, just to entrap them. I summon them now because I need allies. I am a leftover, and thus we are kin.

Slowly, ponderously, a vast shape arises from the sea, and I wade into the waves to greet my lone fellow with open arms.

VOLATILE PATTERNS

BREAKFAST IS MIRACULOUS: OLIVES BAKED INTO SOFT SOURDOUGH BREAD with mayonnaise and egg slices on top, yams cooked in savory sauce, and piping hot blackberry sage tea. My life-partner Mirun beams at me as I praise the food; it all came straight from the fabricator, but during our disastrous visit to Earth, e made sure we'd at least get some good food patterns out of the trip and constantly ran around with a handheld scanner.

"Each new planet strengthens the Alliance, awū Ranai." Mirun quotes the slogan only half-mockingly.

"And indeed," I say. We could use a break, though; the people of Earth have similar bodies to ours here on Eren, but their cognotype distribution is different enough to make interactions somewhat exhausting. And even today, our daughter Birayu woke us early with her cries that she wanted to go and learn from meni Abosana *right now*. At least meni Abosana showed up on schedule, Birayu's small study-group now happily off on a day of learning.

I sip my honey-sweet tea and try to relax.

Mirun bites into eir portion, drops and scatters pieces of egg on eir plate. E frowns and picks them up with eir fingers, drops them again. E looks all too tired too, eir skin even paler than usual, eir small body curled up on itself in eir soft blue robes.

"I had a strange hypnopompic vision earlier," e says. "Quite violent. Someone dying . . . I haven't had any precognitive impressions in a while, but I haven't gotten much sleep in a while either. May I show? It's intense."

I nod as e shares the memory reconstruction.

Fire—flames—scattered cries, someone down below breaking down a door. We need to get them out, but where are they. This place was built before the new regs: how could it ever be compliant, who paid off who to get a permit? I can't think. I kick down a thin divider, and it cracks under my boot, satisfying.

There are coatracks right inside, and they're all on fire, just like downstairs; there must be many separate sources. This is not an accident but arson. I turn around and the coatrack next to me topples. I raise my arm to fend it off, but the coats all fall out and on top of me, the angle is all wrong, the coats wrap around me to blanket me in flame, and it should go out and my suit should be able to take it, but—

It's over, but my emotions will be reverberating for a while. Maybe I shouldn't have watched, but e is right about that particular foreboding sense of the future. I'm contemplating this when I get the call—highest priority, the emergency override passing through all my carefully set Do Not Disturb flags.

The caller has at least granted me the possibility to decline, but when I see his name, I know that we ought to talk. I pull my long overcoat around myself.

Commander Morosewi appears, standing next to our table, his body subtly translucent in that particular way that tells me it's an overlay. He's in the caverns of Ereni Security Headquarters, probably being video-recorded by his room because when he sends his mental image of himself he always wears a cowl in addition to his black uniform.

He glares at me, his pale skull—hairless in the Ereni way—glinting in the artificial light, his sizable jaw tense. The dagger-shaped tattoo on his right cheek and forehead twitches as he blinks.

He barks a greeting, and I return it gracefully. Mirun murmurs something, and he inclines his head toward em too.

Commander Morosewi always seems bothered by the sight of our tiny apartment. Is it because of the warm tones? The hand-carved wood and the blown glass? Certainly, these are indulgences, but Eren is no longer the resource-strapped former mining colony that it used to be.

"Much esteemed Ranai, head of the Iwunen household," he says—just slightly more formal than usual, but I am alarmed. "I'm here to ask for a favor. I know you've just returned from an investigation, but . . ."

I cross my thick arms; I know I can be just as intimidating as he is. "We've done enough for the Alliance for a few months at least. First, the case with that dissident sculptor and then the trip to Earth . . ."

Commander Morosewi looks ill at ease. "This is not for the Alliance. This is for us. I am here on the express request of Supreme Councilor Orowōyā, and I defer to her expertise. She herself will take the time to tell you more if you agree."

Despite myself, I'm interested.

Mirun leans forward, forgetting about eir food. "Is this about the riots on Dehhe?"

Morosewi nods, eyebrows raised. "How did you guess?"

"I was just thinking, there aren't that many countries that Eren has relations with independently of the Alliance, and I read about the situation on Dehhe yesterday in my labor rights feed."

"I should hire you as an analyst one of these days," he says.

Mirun chuckles. "I don't think the esteemed Commander could hire me away from awū Ranai!"

The commander clears his throat. "In any case, Dehhe asked for a team of investigators. They are having unexplained goings-on, and they suspect the riots are part of that."

"How will we be compensated?" Mirun asks the question that has been hovering unspoken in my thoughts. We have everything what we need—except for some well-deserved rest.

Commander Morosewi slowly turns around. "Dehhe has a longstanding tradition of blown glass that some say predates the times of the Old Empire . . ."

This is unlikely, I think, given that Dehhe was probably not even inhabited before the Old Empire, but my curiosity is tickled. "Do you by any chance have pictures?"

We finish our breakfast, and I make a call to the Supreme Councilor. Orowōyā looks as resplendent as ever, the orange and crimson of her robe complementing the deep dark browns of her skin, the undulating, nonfigurative embroidered patterns gently promoting māwal circulation. Orange is for society, connections, ties that bind. Governance. One of the three fundamental colors of the Free State of Eren. Red is not fundamental but important nonetheless: it's associated with power, this particular crimson tone referencing an inclination to subtlety over brute force.

We go through our greetings, comfortable in our formality. "I am truly glad you have agreed to this urgent request," she says and means it. I don't know her well, but we are on friendly terms—of all the Supreme Councilors, she is the most familiar to me.

"I don't know how much Commander Morosewi has explained?" she asks.

"Precious little, Councilor. He said that he deferred to you."

"Defers to me or disclaims responsibility? Well then." She allows amusement to percolate through her features, but then she turns grim. "I myself know little. Dehhe is an important trade partner of ours, and I'm on good terms with Prime Minister Sounhha Sehisran. She said I could share this."

The Councilor gestures in the air, and a recording starts playing; there is no video, just sound. Sounhha Sehisran has a soft but vivacious mezzosoprano voice.

"—and if you could, I've been trying to regard all the misfortune as coincidental, but it's escalating, and some do suspect it's of a"—she hesitates—"magical nature. So far, it's mostly been confined to the capital, but . . . it's starting to crop up in cabinet meetings as well, and I need to reassure my ministers, you understand. I myself am skeptical, but I defer to expert judgment."

Orowōyā waves away the recording and sighs. "All this deference in one day! I grow tired."

Every time we've gone outside Alliance space unprepared, things have gone badly. Now I know to ask a few questions beforehand. "Does the Alliance have any people on the ground?"

She grimaces. "They must do, but I haven't been able to get a contact. Everyone is busy with the Treaty Enforcement scandal over there."

I wince. "I can see that. Eren is a small member state."

"Don't get me wrong. We have plenty of clout," she says. "I don't think they are deliberately withholding intelligence from us. It's just that Alliance Central is busy with its own problems these days. But if you could help us with this . . ."

I raise a hand. "Glass art goes a long way toward ensuring my cooperation."

The spaceport glitters—all too bright, all too white. I adjust my visual input just a little; Ereni standard interfaces have their advantages. The world becomes more bearable. Dehhe is rich, rich enough not to even consider joining the Alliance, and spaceports are locations where states like to showcase their resources.

Mirun spins around, trying to stare at everything at the same time. E topples over our floater-pod, yelps, scrambles up before I can step closer to help em. "Thank you, awū Ranai. I'm fine," e declares all too loudly. Over the years, I've learned that "I'm fine" usually means impending disaster, so I nudge the floater-pod over to my side and firmly steer Mirun away.

I am explicitly awū, the dominant partner in our relationship, and this works out well for both of us. E relaxes a little.

We stand in line. Everyone else seems local. The people of Dehhe all have the same body template, like ours, but their cognotype distribution is more similar to that of Earth. Our beloved Eren is somewhat of an outlier.

The officer who's verifying our hastily issued visas is wearing a garish orange overcoat with embroidery and haphazardly sewn appliqué. The colors and patterns look as if they followed Ereni dress symbolism, but they don't—everything is off, as if I were hearing an unfamiliar language sharing a phonological inventory with a language I speak. The patterns don't make sense, but they *almost* do; the lines of the garment do not channel māwal in the right way.

When the officer takes our biometrics, I notice the scratches on her hands. Doesn't she have self-repair? I hope feral cats are not common here—I still remember my time in the Aruanar Combatspace.

I expect her to say something uncomfortable about our genders, interrogate us whether we are men or women, but she does nothing of the sort. She appears distracted and possibly in pain.

Mirun messages me via our interface.

Awū Ranai, what kind of clothing is that?

I'm glad e noticed it too. Being more observant of our environment is always handy when we are supposed to be investigating a crime. Except there is no crime, just general unrest and politicians with ample strings to pull.

No one is waiting for us. Our lodgings are just outside the spaceport, and we've been instructed to follow the red lines. Mirun runs around cheerfully and points out details that likely have no bearing whatsoever on our investigation. It's comforting that at least one of us feels capable of doing this after a trip across many jump points and a never-ending flight on a passenger liner leaving Alliance space, while reassuring Birayu over video that, yes, we will be back soon, and Anayāun-mowi will take her to the vegetable gardens in the evening.

The wave of raw emotion hits us in synch with the cold air when we step outside. We are swept away by the demonstrating crowd. The translation subroutines of my interface struggle with all the concurrent noisy input. Signs flicker from Ereni to Dehxen and back when I crane my neck around. I need to be back on Eren where my interface can rely on the local network. I need to be someplace else, very fast, because this chaos is the last thing I need right now—

"—say we can burn, burn, burn 'em down—"

"Nem hagy-juk!"

"For the laborers, for the laborers! For life!"

"Solidarity means resistance! Kam defahi im—"

People of all shapes and sizes surround us. I don't know much about the local ethnoracial groupings, but I can parse out at least three different clusters. Everyone seems united in fury, running themselves ragged, their clothes torn.

I take a deep abdominal breath, pulling the smells of sweat and anger into myself. Exhaling them. I strengthen my wards with the motion. Then I grab Mirun's arm: e's entranced by the crowd.

"Are these the riots you mentioned?" I yell.

"Awūn-ē, this is just a small demonstration—" e yells back, then the first large object whizzes past my ears, crashing into an advertising display. Sparks fly. The display screams "ENCHANTING EMBROIDERY!! SURPRISE YOUR SWEETHRRRG" and then it fizzles out. The crowd roars in unison.

"Let's get out of here before the cops show up," I shout. Fortunately for both of us, Mirun is skilled in much besides keeping tabs on labor rights activism in far-off countries. E pulls me down to a crouch, twists and turns, and in just three implausibly long steps, we are out of the clash. Mirun learned from me, but I couldn't have done this better myself.

We find ourselves standing right in front of another guard in a garish uniform who stares at us and can only mutter, "Magic."

Mirun shrugs. "Matter displacement. Or technically, a shortening of distances. Nice to meet you?"

"You are the wizards?" the guard asks, oddly relieved. As his facial muscles relax, I notice a set of vertical scratches on his face and neck that end at his embroidered collar. "I've been looking for you."

The translation seems antiquated. "Wizards?"

"Magicians, witches. Bastard offspring."

I am about 99 percent sure the guard did not mean to say "bastard offspring."

"We are the investigators from the Free State of Eren, yes." I don't think our specific terminology would make it across the translation gap, so instead of *māwalēni*, I just repeat what he said, with slight unease. "Wizards."

He's delighted, which is unexpected; in a language that has *magicians* and *bastard offspring* as distant synonyms, I would not expect to get a warm welcome. But cultural trends change fast.

"I'm so glad to meet you," he says. "I was sent to pick you up when the PM's office realized you'd be arriving in the middle of the newest demonstrations. You can drop your gear in your lodgings later. PM Sehisran is waiting for you."

Something must be really wrong if she's so ready to meet us. Mirun passes me a startled glance. But onward we go.

The officer steps back, greets the two other guards by the immense carved entrance to the PM's office.

Sounhha Sehisran hurries to the door to welcome us in herself, and my breath stops.

She is a short, stolid-appearing woman with round features, light brown skin the exact shade of mine, and wavy black hair that's chopped short just below her ears. She looks trustworthy, in a way that probably makes constituents flock to her, and canny enough to lead an entire planet.

She is wearing a wonderfully intricate, richly embroidered bright-orange Ereni dress.

She notices my attention in the way of someone accustomed to it. "Oh, my dress? It was a personal gift from Supreme Councilor Orowōyā after the latest round of the trade negotiations."

And fitted to her personally, no doubt. It's not only a perfect size and shape, but I can also feel that all the embroidery and appliqué and cord serve to guide Sounhha Sehisran's natural māwal in a harmonic way. She would be charismatic without it, but with it, the effect is simply stunning.

I nod in appreciation but also in mounting worry. "It's beautiful," I say. "Truly a gift fit for a ruler."

And appropriate too: the designs clearly mark the *dress* as Ereni but *her* as a foreign ruler. We have very delicate symbolism and a tradition of gifting handicrafts to dignitaries, though they usually end up in a museum on display. I can't fault her for wearing her own dress, but it feels slightly like a faux pas, and I'm not sure why. Mirun also looks uneasy, but Mirun always looks uneasy, especially when we go off-planet. I need a moment to think this over, but PM Sehisran doesn't allow me a pause—not even to examine the majestic yellow glass vase on her massive desk of solid wood, both designed in the style of quasi-organic abstraction.

"You will be able to accompany me to my next cabinet meeting, starting in just a few minutes," she says. "We can drink a cup of hot saba juice and then we must be on our way."

Mirun almost drops the cup that PM Sehisran presses into eir hands. E takes a sip gingerly and makes a face; I know that feeling when self-repair tries to fix a scalded tongue. E valiantly downs the entire cup. I also taste mine. It's not so hot, but then again, my heat tolerance is very high. I'm thinking we might need it as PM Sehisran ushers us next door into a room full of shouting people.

The sight is astounding. In the spacious, eggshell-colored meeting room, there are about a dozen scratched and battered people, some even bleeding from small but fresh cuts. They are also wearing the most outrageous garments. Where the guards' haphazardly assembled costumes were simply garish, these are eye-gouging.

PM Sehisran smiles, embarrassed. "I seem to have started a trend," she says.

Mirun grins and messages me via my interface. *Awū Ranai, I do believe we've solved the case?*

I steel myself and message back. *We've solved the case, but yet again, we haven't solved the problem.*

When the ministers notice us, they jump to their feet, knocking against the oversized round table. An athletic-looking white man gets so close to me that Mirun holds out an arm to warn him off. He steps back but continues yelling. "You need to figure out what's going on! You're the experts! We've been cursed!" He spreads his arm in desperation, and his suit rips in half, showing his shaved and waxed abdomen.

I clap my hands three times to quiet the noise, and I put just a bit of māwal into the sound so that it would carry over the shouting. The ministers fall silent, but some are still so angry they are visibly shaking.

"Awū Ranai, if I may?" Mirun asks, and I motion em forward.

"You haven't been cursed," Mirun says. "Your issue is simple, and it traces back to the Prime Minister's clothes." E pauses, looks if they are following. There are sporadic nods around the table. "I'm also certain you could have solved it already if you deigned to ask your own experts."

"What experts?" a thin, dark-skinned woman asks, barely over her breath.

Mirun furrows eir brow, and I know e's searching eir sensory logs for the exact word that would translate. "Wizards," e finally says.

Another round of yelling erupts.

PM Sehisran slaps her palms on the table. "Enough. You know I am a skeptic above all. I don't care what the Ereni do and how they explain it, but they are the experts."

A skeptic? Note the word choice, I message Mirun. *This planet is not such a low-māwal area to allow plausible skepticism. Have there been fluctuations in māwal levels recently?*

Mirun responds, *The Alliance should have that data on file if they really have people on the ground, but we don't. Still, that would be a reasonable guess.*

"Allow me to explain," e says to PM Sehisran's cabinet. "These garments are carefully designed to guide the wearer's . . . magic, if you will. The lines and patterns are not arbitrary. Improvising on them without being aware of the design principles is . . . not going to be fruitful."

I also step in, seeing an opening to tie the abstract to the personal. "Do your clothes scratch you when you put them on, take them off? Do they tear? Do the zippers catch at your skin? Do your wounds not heal?"

Nods around the table.

I cede the floor to Mirun again. E goes on without missing a beat; we work well together. "You all tried to one-up each other and have the most gorgeous design approximating the Prime Minister's garments, but the clothes work well for her not because an Ereni artisan has gone overboard with embroidery but because what there is works well with her natural magic. You are locked in a positive feedback loop, a runaway reaction where, the more and more dramatic your garments, the more likely you think they are going to increase your station—but instead the more havoc they cause. Without you even realizing." E sighs. "These patterns work. Their distorted versions also work—and produce further distortion."

I wonder how much of this made it across intact with our imperfect translation software, but whispers and half-sentences start up around the table. "Then the riots?" "They did start in the textile industry . . ." "The burning factories?"

I pounce on the words. "*What* has been burning?"

Mirun gasps as e connects the dots. "But of course! The factories—many clothes with the same patterns and combined with an atmosphere of grievance— your workers aren't paid that well, are they?"

A minister stands, pulls herself up to full height, shaking with anger. "If you are accusing us of sweatshop labor—"

This isn't going to end well. I raise my hands. "No one is accusing anyone of anything. But for now, it would be best if production of these . . . garments could be halted. For purely safety reasons."

"These are privately owned enterprises we are talking about!" a man yells and slams a fist on the table. "We can't just shut them down with, what, riot police?"

I also raise my voice. "If you don't shut them down with riot police or whatever else you have, you might need to shut them down with firefighters and emergency medics. What has burned down already?"

PM Sehisran grits her teeth and looks away, probably accessing her interface; I'm not sure what is standard on Dehhe.

She hisses softly; then she curses.

"I can't send this to you, some kind of incompatibility," she says and steps to a wall. "But I can project it."

We see a tall, cuboid building with tiny windows that explode outward as we watch. A deep voice comments. "That's not glass. That's heat-resistant plastic."

A minister asks, "Is this ongoing right now?" PM Sehisran nods, mutters agreement.

The minister who's still standing whispers, "This should not be happening."

"Do we have a video feed from inside?" I ask.

The deep voice says, "I have some from a helmet cam."

With my feet rooted to the floor, but hopelessly unrooted on this foreign planet, I watch as I see the familiar images play out: a bulky firefighter raising her arm as a flaming coatrack topples on her and the suits twist and bend around her, trying to suffocate.

The feed cuts out.

"There are still firefighters inside—and workers," the deep voice explains. "All the equipment outside is broken. They can't get the jets working."

I snap my head to Mirun. "We need to ward it. All this disturbance . . ." I don't need to explain. We are working on it already, reaching out with our minds across the distance. It doesn't seem very far actually.

"Where is this place?" I ask. "How fast can we get there?"

PM Sehisran smiles dryly, and a wall rolls away. Behind it, there is a set of floor-to-ceiling glass panes, and beyond that is the capital, smoke rising in the distance.

"I've always wanted a good enough reason to do that," she says.

Mirun glances out, eir mind half-occupied by the warding. E speaks slowly. "I'd rather not fly. We'll need all our energy once we get there. Maybe a ride?"

PM Sehisran is confused for a moment, and I know she didn't realize at first that we can fly under our own power if we must. There is enough ambient māwal for that, but just barely. It's a stretch. And right now, we can't be thinly stretched if we want to make any difference. She nods.

"I can offer my own transport. I've always wanted a good enough reason to do *this* too," she says as a vehicle descends—probably from the roof—and hovers by the windowpane. PM Sehisran slides away the pane and steps into the transport. There is no wind; there must be a force field around the building, the vehicle, or both.

I gently guide Mirun into the transport; eir focus is at the building site.

The standing minister yells. "I'm also coming! I'm the Minister of Infrastructure, I need to be there!"

I get the sense there must be some kind of rivalry between her and Sounhha Sehisran. It's not my concern.

"Come then," PM Sehisran says with just a touch of weariness.

It takes just a few minutes for us to arrive, speeding across the evening sky toward the sinking sun. The building is already assailed by jets of water; our wards have taken hold, and the firefighting equipment is operational again.

Mirun shakes eir head to clear it for the next task. I must go in—ostensibly to gather evidence, to convince the skeptics. Honestly, I just want to make sure we get the remaining workers and firefighters out. I have never been afraid of being burned, and I have more than enough māwal to keep harm at bay.

"You can help me sustain my defenses," I say. "From *outside*. This is not an argument."

E nods. We hug; we kiss. Then I run into the factory, my power hastening my steps. The ground floor is occupied by rows upon rows of broken fabricators, and I pass them quickly by, make my way upstairs where the more valuable handmade garments are produced. I run into storage room after storage room, open a cabinet only to have half a dozen garments fall on me, try to attach themselves to me, bounce off my shields.

This is not going to help. How am I to carry them? I make the back hemisphere of my shield sticky and throw the flailing garments into the air. I run again, a wobbly layer of clothing behind me. I've been experimenting with making my shields spin, as a form of active defense, but I need to keep my field of view clear of flapping shirt-arms and unraveling threads of embroidery.

I dash into a larger hall, full of fabric in a roiling, sparkling heap. If there is a critical mass of angry māwal-active objects, this is it.

I roar like a bear, my shout shaking the air, and the fabrics separate, scatter against the walls. The ambient māwal calms down a little. The sparks subside. I take a deep breath and send the last few minutes of my sensory stream to Mirun outside; we need a backup in case something goes wrong. Because of this boneheaded need for *proof.*

Behind a door in another hallway, I find the unlucky firefighter trapped under the rack. She does not seem badly burned, but she's unconscious and will not rouse. I drag her up and back across corridors upon corridors. Anger fuels my strength. All this could have been avoided. All this.

Outside, I hand her to the emergency responders, and without losing speed, I turn to PM Sehisran and her circle of onlookers. "You want proof? I'll give you proof!" I yell and shoot straight up into the air, drawing on the raw strength of the flames, my own anger and that accumulated in the garments, from frustrated and tired and annoyed and fuming and raging laborers urged on by supervisors desperate to fill the sudden demand for the newfangled foreign fashion.

I rise, spreading my arms.

I soar past floors upon floors of chaos, land on the roof. A small group of people are trapped up there, waiting for a rescue. Where *is* the rescue?

I ping Mirun, and e shouts at PM Sehisran until the ministerial transport takes to the skies again, and I watch as the last of the begrimed, soot-covered laborers and the bone-weary firefighters stumble into the pristine interior of the vehicle. I can't help feeling glee, a rare emotion, and feeling that justice is being served—even as I know that the interior probably has enough nanites to gobble up and reprocess an entire truckload of soot in a matter of minutes.

PM Sehisran will get a great photo op out of this.

I can't sense anyone else still in the building, but I ask Mirun to make sure before I spread my arms out again and jump.

It must be the anger clouding my mind.

I misjudge my power.

My smooth glide turns into freefall.

My eyes lock on PM Sehisran as her mouth opens in a desperate scream. I shouldn't see such small details from so high up, but I do.

It must be the fear.

"Awūn-ē!" Mirun shouts and pushes me upward with a burst of raw māwal. My robes and all the ravenous garments I'm still dragging behind myself billow out toward the sky.

It's not the smoothest landing, but I manage.

"Are you satisfied?" I groan at the prime minister's entourage. Mirun trundles toward me on unsteady feet. We hold each other close for a long moment before we separate again—for my turn to yell.

"If you wanted safe patterns, you could have asked! These are formal, ceremonial garments!" I point at PM Sehisran and sweep my arm back in an arc, disabling my shields. The clothing items plop to the ground in time to punctuate my words. "*These* are misguided imitations."

Mirun adds, "You will want to destroy them quickly."

I sigh. "And hire a Cultural Interchange team next."

PM Sehisran glares. At this moment, I realize there are many ways of creating a position ruling an entire planet, but very few of them are peaceful. Even if she's doing her best. Even if she was elected to her position. I don't know the history, but I know power, and I know temptation.

I push my excess anger into the pile of clothes and turn around to watch the sparks take to the air from the impromptu pyre.

I cough and turn back to PM Sehisran.

I must calm myself.

"I believe we were discussing traditional glass art," I say.

Birayu looks at the yellow glass vase, its soaring arcs and undulating lines pitch-perfect in the style of quasi-organic abstraction.

She tilts her head to the side and frowns.

Objects hold their histories, and I'm wondering what she senses. Then she turns around and marches back to the fabricator to make a set of six rainbow cupcakes.

THE LADYBUG, IN FLIGHT

for Katalina

IT IS GOOD TO BE SMALL; IT IS GOOD TO BE MANY.

A hundred, a thousand, five thousand. We swarm where we can find nourishment—and because we are constructs, nourishment is inorganic.

We gobble up space crystals; we shine our beam of light on time crystals to get the process in motion and feed on the oscillations.

Do you know about symmetry breaking? These crystals have less symmetry than a glop of liquid.

But of course, I'm just a tiny ladybug—my brain quasi-organic, my outer layers made of a curious alloy. My sentience forming from the swarm.

And we are often hungry.

There are entire ecosystems in space. Near the planets with nurseries where the large sentient ships grow, there is enough crystal crumble to support us, so the ships can feed on the output of our digestive processes.

Preferably not on us.

That's after they're grown; when they are growing, they feed on people.

I am told the people like it.

Sometimes, we chance upon nonsentient ships, chunks of metal or plastic, floating aimlessly. That's when we get to work. We know how to use an airlock if we find one; we know how to find breaches in the hull if we don't. If our swarm is big enough, we know how to circumvent conventional physics, teleport inside.

Sometimes, we find people alive, like you. Usually when we do, they don't attempt to talk. We are practiced at communicating without appearing to communicate. We are often not given the benefit of doubt.

Unlike this time, and thus, now we are cheerful.

I am inordinately happy when someone comments on my spots.

You are a small human, but that's all right. When you grow up, the ships can feed on you. If you want to try.

That's not the real reason why I guide you back to Alliance space.

You can look around, but there's only one of me inside; the hull of your ship remains sturdy. We could not force our way in, and teleporting takes a lot of effort.

If you can find the right camera output, you will see us swarming outside. I think we are beautiful, but you humans think your own nonsentient ships are beautiful. Clearly our standpoints are different.

But you like my spots. You might like this too.

I am sorry the others are unconscious. You are an exception, maybe in more ways than one.

Maybe the others won't like us. There is always an element of risk involved.

It's also a lot of effort to guide a ship home. But we are likewise searching, and it might help us too—to come along for the ride.

We were all made by the Empire Long Gone. We do not mourn empires; their names show us the original intent behind creating them. We aren't invaders.

We only entered the ship because we were worried for you.

We aren't tasty. This you'll have to believe because I don't have any energy left to initiate my toxic spray, designed for emergency self-defense. It can use up to 10 percent of our body fluids, and I already used up close to 20 just to come inside.

I'm glad you don't want to eat me. I'm glad we can clear up misunderstandings, even if you don't understand all my words.

You will remember me when you grow.

Will you miss me? We miss them, all the people we met back in the day. Even the humans.

We liked knowing the people of the silver barrel. They also weren't strictly organic or inorganic really. They had human shapes, but they could change. Into swarms, even; this meant they could understand us. We miss them.

Will you let me sit on your shoulder?

I'm tired. I'm also searching for home.

If I take you to your home, maybe you can help me find mine. Home is other people, I heard the humans say—or maybe I misunderstood.

Yes, your humans. We felt the vibrations through your ship's hull, and we have long since learned your language.

If we hurry up, your other humans will probably be able to wake up again.

In the meanwhile, I'll sit on your shoulder like this, and now you can sing me that song, the one you've been mentioning. About the ladybug in flight.

I'll tell you the coordinates to input.

THE 1ST INTERSPECIES SOLIDARITY FAIR AND PARADE

I.

Name: Rita M.
Age: 16
Occupation: Farmworker

I FILL OUT THE SPREADSHEET PINNED TO ONE OF THOSE ANTIQUATED clip-on boards. "Now I'll ask you a few questions that might seem unrelated." I start going through my usual script. "The screening will take approximately ten minutes."

Rita M. looks at me flatly, gives me the yet-another-clueless-adult glance. "It's pointless," she says. "I don't want to be recruited."

This is the third time someone has turned me down today, and it's barely afternoon. My stomach clenches. We don't have time for this. We'll never fill our recruitment quota like this.

"That's fine," I say, and I somehow manage to keep my calm. "I'm not going to force you. Provide a reason, and I'll put it in the spreadsheet, save you the hassle next time a recruiter comes around."

She shrugs slowly as if her two thick brown braids were weighing down her whole body. "Mom and Dad need me on the farm. We're barely making do as is, and Mr. Hodász no longer takes the eggs and the corn." Another shrug. "I'm also not really interested in the aliens."

I believe her. All throughout our conversation, she never once glanced at the giant metallic sphere hovering next to me.

The two of us are taking one of the backcountry roads between farms—what used to be Győr-Moson-Sopron county back when Hungary still existed. Everything's almost entirely deserted; all the time we walk, we only meet one person going in the opposite direction, a dirt-smeared teen carrying a shovel. I stare downward because I keep on slipping in the mud, but there's not much scenery to look at anyway. A weeping willow by the wayside, a crumbling stone cross, and once something that looks like an oversize bomb crater, somehow still not overgrown with weeds after so many years. Lukrécia floats next to me, sparing me the commentary. I'm angry and sad: angry that no one wants to be recruited for the alien communication team, sad because I see their reasons. Everyone is exhausted. After the first group of aliens destroyed everything almost two decades ago and the second group came to pick up the scraps, no one trusts that the third group is actually friendly. Even though they are not a singular empire or even the same species. They are of a wide variety of species and origin, and the only thing that binds them together is that their planets had been invaded like ours—by the same aliens as ours. Yet no one believes that, this time, we're all in this together. No one wants to come work with us. But we need to talk to each other, we need to find ways—we need to recruit more people . . .

After a while, I get frustrated enough that I start up a conversation myself.

"Do you think we'll find a candidate today? Not even an actual recruit, just someone we can take back to base for a longer evaluation?"

Lukrécia meows. She has this idea that humans will relate to her better if she pretends to be a cat from an eighties cartoon. I don't know how to tell her that this didn't work out for the second round of aliens either. It has all been tried.

"Is that a yes or a no?" I grump at her.

"Neither," she says, her voice level. "It's an answer to a badly posed question."

She's so much out of character as a cat that I can't help snorting with amusement. "Lukrécia. You're a giant sphere, not a cartoon cat."

"I'm not a sphere. The sphere is my containment unit."

"I'm just telling you how you come across to people." I poke at her containment unit and almost fall over as I slip again. I could use better boots. I could use a different life, one with well-maintained roads.

"They're remarkably uncurious about me," Lukrécia says.

Now I'm angry with her too. "They're trying to stay alive. Give them some credit. They'd be curious if they had a moment of respite from all that labor, just a *moment* really. We're a distraction."

We trundle in silence for a few minutes. The next time, I'm not the one who speaks up. "Do you think we should go into the city?" Lukrécia asks. If she's already buying into the human stereotypes about farmers and rural people, I'll be tempted to throttle her nonexistent neck.

I shake my head. My anger will not serve any purpose here. Not anymore. *Those* aliens are gone. "I already made the rounds with Bubó," I say. "They couldn't spare anyone from the rebuilding."

She meows. "I don't mean Pannonhalma. I don't mean the town. I mean Győr. *The city.*"

I have approximately one hundred counterarguments. It's far. It's dangerous. The city is full of uncleared rubble and groups of militants. I will fall and injure myself, and we won't be able to get help. We won't be able to recruit among the scavengers. They'll try to hurt us. I will fall.

But we are sadly behind quota. No one from the farms or even the neighboring town of Pannonhalma wants to be recruited for extraterrestrial communications. I feel the quotas are unfair, but I'm terrible at management—and if I complain, people will just say, "If you know it so well, organize it yourself."

I take a deep breath: it comes out more like a gasp than a sigh. "Tell you what. We do this last remaining farm today. There's an inn in Győrújbarát, they're renting out the cabins up the hillside, the old summer camp." Lukrécia doesn't protest. I go on. "We stay there tonight. Then we swing around, and maybe we can get into the city from the west-southwest, following the river. Avoid the areas to the south."

"That sounds good," Lukrécia says, understanding the unspoken meaning better than some humans would: despite the anger that drives me forward, I don't want to walk anymore today. My joints are feeling the strain. One sprain too many, one fracture too many. I'm just past thirty-five, but I also get injured more than most people. My ankles are shot for the remainder of my life, my knees hurt, and the only reason I'm out here and not back on base is that they had absolutely no one to spare—with new ships arriving daily.

"There is a paved road," she adds. "From Győrújbarát all the way up to Győr." Is she being conciliatory? It's hard to tell. Her Hungarian is smooth and with a TV anchor accent—if we still had TV. But her emotions are a puzzle to me.

When I don't respond, she goes on. "We can walk comfortably all the way to the city outskirts and try to cross the garden parcels to the river, head to the old freeway. Then we can just walk in. The road's wide enough to avoid an ambush."

"You've done this before."

"No, but that looks like the most reasonable route."

I'm not about to argue with her. I nod at the barns in the distance with my chin. "This one farm, and then we go to the old summer camp, get a good night's sleep."

Name: Bálint P.
Age: 22
Occupation: Farmworker, mechanic

"Will the aliens come and help me get some of the tractors in working order?"

"That's why we're trying to set up ways of collaborati—"

"Can they come tomorrow? This week, at least? Can your friend over there help me get some spare parts? No? Tell me when they can help me out, and I'll see how I can help them out. I can't just go off to Pannonhalma on a whim. I'm needed here!"

Name: Andrea J.
Age: 21
Occupation: Innkeeper

"You know what? I'd love to, but then who'll run the inn? My elderly grandmother? The cabins are up on the hillside, if you didn't come when you were a kid." She tosses a key at me and glares at Lukrécia. At least she doesn't ignore the alien like most everyone today, except the angry mechanic.

I'm not looking forward to the steps, but at least there are steps. And in reasonably good repair too. Someone with a rake is sitting by the side, probably one of the staff taking a break: someone in her late teens, I think. We nod each other a quick greeting and turn away. Surprisingly, the A-frame cabins look like they were renovated since my last time here—for summer camp in elementary school, just after second grade. Well before the first aliens came, when I was already a teen. But inside, the furniture is a hodgepodge, probably gathered from the village of Győrújbarát at the foot of the hills. Everything that wasn't blown to smithereens: glazed wooden cabinets from the Socialist years, a table that was clearly built for outdoor use, school chairs, and a designer sofa that must have been pricy back in the day. I resist checking for a tag.

Lukrécia barely fits through the entrance. I kick off my boots and throw myself down on the sofa. At least we're not sharing with anyone else tonight.

An eight-bed cabin and no one wants to spend a night with the alien.

"You've been here before. Is that correct?"

"Yeah. As a little girl." I turn on my left side. Lukrécia is hovering next to my bed. Her closeness doesn't bother me, and I'm too achy to sleep yet.

"What was it like?" she asks.

"Terrible. I hated it!" I pause. "Fine. I liked the swimming pool."

"There is a swimming pool?"

"Down there," I make a vague gesture. "They might not have it anymore." I think back. "You know what, maybe I didn't like the swimming pool either . . . I liked the water. But the kids made fun of me. That I was too clumsy. I don't know. One of the girls stole my enameled ring, and I cried for hours." This is not the conversation that will help me calm down and fall asleep.

"I'm sorry they made fun of you," Lukrécia says. She's never made fun of me. Ever. I wonder if she knows how. She probably does: her species is cognitively the most similar to humans, out of all the new arrivals. If all of them were like her, we wouldn't need to run around trying to recruit communications specialists.

"Thank you, Lukrécia. That's nice of you to say."

I'm sure people make fun of her. Of me. Behind our backs. But they're also afraid. The first time aliens showed up, they bombed everything. The second time aliens showed up, they were scavengers coming in to exploit a people left vulnerable, a people whose willingness to fight they underestimated. The third time . . .

The third time was, "Hi, we've also been bombed by the people who bombed you. Maybe we could work together, become friends?"

A lot of humans didn't trust that. Especially as more and more aliens showed up in scraggly, beat-up spaceships; aliens of all shapes and sizes and species. Aliens who communicated by affecting the electromagnetic fields near your brain. Aliens who lived on the bodies of other aliens. Aliens who tried to convince humans that all magic was technology or all technology was magic, and then we all went down an endless rabbit hole of translation and mistranslation. A group expressed their wish of converting to Judaism. Another group asked if they could, kindly and consensually, chew on humans' hair. All of them were very enthusiastic about the fact that humans somehow managed to get rid of two waves of invaders, even though no one quite understood how. (Except maybe me and my boundless anger.)

By the time I get to the aliens who look like vintage Modernist carpets from Sweden, I finally drift off to sleep.

Name: Veronika B.

Age: 72

Occupation: Innkeeper (retired)

"Yes, I'm interested in filling out the form," the elderly lady says. She has to be Andrea's grandmother.

"Would you be able to get to the base? We sadly don't have much by way of transportation," I try to sound more apologetic than combative. I did not sleep well. All that soreness.

"My dear husband has a carriage and two horses," she says. I perk up. Wouldn't the horses be missed here? A carriage is a veritable asset. But I just nod as if I heard a variant on this every day.

"I'll ask you a few questions then."

She reaches out for my clip-on board. "I know what a survey form is. Just give it to me, and I'll tick the boxes for you." She sighs. "Before the invasion, I used to be a sociologist."

Oh.

I hand her the board. I wonder if she also speaks foreign languages.

"Here you go." That was fast. She blinks at me. "How do you score this?"

I shrug. "By this point I have it all memorized."

"Ha! You can tell at a glance. I remember those days." She grins.

I look down on the sheet of paper, printed on both sides. I flip it around. Openness to experience, sensation-seeking . . . in these screenings, we are trying to measure who would be good at talking to the aliens. I barely have to look at her choices to know she's a solid pick.

She chuckles. "You know, I can guess what those items measure, and I can give you any desired score."

I grin back at her, finally more at ease. "That in itself would probably make you a good candidate."

Lukrécia purrs.

The retired innkeeper and her husband are not interested in driving into Győr with us on the carriage; besides, they have to pack up their entire lives. They know the way to Pannonhalma, and the base is at the foot of the hill. They haven't seen the base before, but it's hard to miss with all the landers parked around it. We say goodbye, and off we go on a cracked and occasionally caved-in but mercifully paved road, snaking toward the north. So far, so good. But we are still low on potential recruits, the base is understaffed, and everything is kind of falling apart. I'm glad I don't know what's going on back there, though I had such a weird dream last night, and I can't help wondering if that in itself was a communication attempt. It involved three aliens of different species chasing each other in a circle while screaming incomprehensibly.

We get to the southern outskirts of the city in good time, and we stop to stare at the ten-story concrete housing blocks. Someone passes us, walking in the opposite direction with brisk steps. I gaze at the buildings and try not to look like someone clearly not from here. Not any longer.

"You know, those blocks were supposed to last only for fifty years or so," I say. "They look in pretty good shape still."

"Some are inhabited," Lukrécia says. "You can see the laundry hung to dry."

I glare at the balconies, only open to one side. I can't quite see anything. Maybe a little movement, a flutter here and there. "If you say so."

"Should we go in?"

There is a veritable moat dug around the blocks of Communist-era housing. "I don't think we can cross that." I don't want to reproach Lukrécia, but she can float while I can barely walk. For the umpteenth time, I fantasize about affixing a chair to the top of her sphere. Knowing my balance, I would probably fall off around the first corner. People say motor dyspraxia improves with age, but I feel like that's counterbalanced by the amount of injuries I acquired throughout the years that never quite healed right.

Maybe it will all be different now. We'll have hospitals again. City centers clear of rubble.

Once we manage to convince all the aliens. The humans too.

At least Lukrécia is convinced. "Then we'll go by the original plan and skirt the city around the west side."

More mud and treacherous terrain. At least the fences have by and large disintegrated with age, though there's always the odd chain-link that threatens to give me tetanus. I can't recall when I last had a booster shot. Before the first wave of aliens came.

"Let's go," I nod to the left, toward the mass of small parcels of land lying fallow, gardens gone to seed, the occasional storage shed or vacation cottage. I reach into a side pocket for my fraying gloves. "You take point."

It's easier going than I'd expected, but my expectations were low. Lukrécia simply pushes over the occasional fence with the bulk of her containment unit, and then I can tiptoe over the remains. There is a waist-high jumble of plants in places: bushes gone wild, determined perennials coming up year after year even with no one taking care of them anymore, invasives finally having free rein. But I'm used to that and mercifully not allergic to ragweed, so I just stumble across the plots in my usual way, following Lukrécia. I'll have to check for ticks when we get to a place I can undress; I don't think any part of me is exposed besides my face, but they are sneaky little things, and I don't think I'm up to explaining Lyme disease or tick-borne encephalitis to Lukrécia.

I find myself wondering if her giant sphere is resistant to bullets.

II.

We don't come across anyone until we're almost to the city, out on the freeway. I peel burrs off my camo fatigues and mentally praise the Bundeswehr for their clothing that lasts absolutely forever. I don't think Germany exists anymore either; Austria certainly doesn't. But these camo fatigues survive. My knees are burning with pain. I sometimes feel that my pants will last longer than me.

We get to a barricade only when we're almost downtown, next to the old Science Education Society building.

"Hey, you. You there," someone yells from the top and clambers over using handholds I can't quite see. The sun's already set, and it's getting dark.

"You're the person who's been following us," Lukrécia notes, detached as usual.

Someone's been following us? "You could've thought to mention that," I groan at her. So much for alien communication. So much for me understanding Lukrécia or her understanding me.

The person chuckles, pulls back their hat, and I realize we've met them at least three times already, always carrying a different implement. I feel that made them invisible to me, and I look away, ashamed. They laugh.

"I'm Lala," they say, and that's a boys' name, though I'm not entirely certain about Lala's gender.

"From *Fairy Lala*?" Lukrécia asks.

"*Humans* are not named after children's shows," I groan at the alien.

"From *Fairy Lala* indeed," Lala grins at us. "I wish I could watch the TV movie. The older people told me all about it. But the book was awesome."

I want to recruit him. It's not just because he could follow us without me noticing. I'm not the most perceptive person, especially when I'm spending three-quarters of my brain resources on not falling flat on my face in the mud. It's not just because of the modern classic about the young fairy prince with the human heart. It's because he comes across as cunning. Cunning *and* cheerful. Unlike me, the angry grouch.

I mutter something about the fairy X-ray machine scene in the book, and he laughs some more. Is he stalling for time? Waiting for an armed squad of scavengers to get to us? Waiting for his backup?

"You know why we're here," I say. I'm bluffing, but he has to know.

"Yeah, but I don't trust you," he replies offhand. "I'll let you pass, and we have a place you can crash too. But I don't know who'd follow you to Pannonhalma."

He turns back toward the barricade and opens a door—makeshift but with a proper lock. He ushers us through, and I can feel his gaze burning at my back.

I'm suddenly not sure who's doing the observing and recruiting here.

Inside, everything is remarkably tidy. Saint Stephen Road looks carefully swept, and someone planted flowers in the divider strip, almost like before. People nod at Lala as we pass by. Many of them openly stare at Lukrécia, but they don't seem hostile.

I'm struck by how varied a bunch they are only after a few minutes, when I almost bump into a Jewish man in Chasidic garb, with side-curls. How did they get here? Chasidic Jews didn't live in Győr before the invasion. My one Jewish classmate complained that everyone in town was so secular, that there were enough people for the community prayers only once a year, when families visited from Israel and the US for Holocaust Memorial Day.

I look around more bravely. I notice that the kids playing a very intricate version of hopscotch are Romani, two elderly women sitting on a bench are talking in a Slavic language—probably Slovakian?—and a man tells his dog to back off from Lukrécia in German.

"Wow, this is how Győr must have looked before the war." I tell Lukrécia. Or no one in particular.

"Before the invasion?" she asks.

"No, the *war*." I pause. "World War II."

Mercifully, she doesn't ask me to clarify.

We are led to the old hotel on the corner of Baross Street. I never thought I'd stay there. It looks much dingier now but, overall, not in terrible shape. I feel like a visiting dignitary.

I'm sure we are being overheard, but I don't care. I want to sleep, but I also want to talk to Lukrécia.

"I think they're spreading the rumors that Győr is a devastated hellscape so that people don't come to snoop," I tell her. I'm not sure how I feel about it. There are plenty of people in the countryside who could use a place like this but somehow got left out when communication was disrupted. For every ethnic group I saw inside, there were people I saw outside, separate and lonely. *I* could use a place like this, and I'm an ethnic majority Hungarian. Not that Hungary is still around.

I try to refocus on what I have for now. I stretch out on the bed, nice and clean after a shower. I can't believe there's running water here, though the water pressure's terribly low.

"Why did they let us in?" Lukrécia asks.

I shrug. "For all I know, they're spying on us. Gathering intelligence."

Before I fall asleep, I wonder yet again—why do I even bother talking to the aliens? I used to think because I was from the last generation who grew up on sci-fi. But Lala read *Fairy Lala* . . .

Lala joins us for breakfast in the dining hall.

"What is this?" I poke at the flat brown . . . thing in the middle of my plate, smeared with some kind of light-yellowish . . . thing.

"Fried eggplant," he chuckles. "With tahini sauce."

That's very much not a Hungarian food, though I'm sure eggplant grows here just fine. I wonder if Lala is Jewish too; his hair is curly and dark. I feel bad about my instantaneous reaction to ethnically profile him. I'm twice his age. He's never known the country the way it was. He never had video games and social media and terrible national politics. I'm the sensible, responsible adult. If he's Jewish, so what? I'm disabled.

The eggplant tastes great, and I shovel it in with relish. I dab at my mouth with a fabric square; it's fancy if a bit faded after many washings. I blink at Lala. *Is* he Jewish?

"If you're trying to guess whether I'm trans, I'll save you the time," he says, grinning broadly. "I am."

I could sink under the floor in shame. I mutter some kind of apology, which only makes Lala grin even more. I need to change the topic fast.

"How come you never saw all this from above?" I ask Lukrécia. "The town is clearly inhabited, and you have aircraft. You can fly."

"It appears we have much more to learn about human habitation patterns," she says. "We saw. We just didn't understand."

Lala chuckles, pokes at his own food with a slightly out-of-shape fork, something from a school dining hall rather than the formerly posh hotel. "We're trying to hide as much as we can. Food supply is tricky. We trade a lot. One of our main procurers vanished recently, and we're all starting to get concerned."

I heard something about this in the villages. "Mr. Hodász?"

He drops the fork with a clang. "You know him?"

"I talked to a lot of farmers lately. I haven't met him." Lala picks up the fork. I feel like I'm a constant source of disappointment. The responsible adult! I sigh. "The farmers miss him too."

I steel myself and go on. "We need to work together somehow. We came here to get some of you to work *for* us. But we'd rather work *with* you. And the villagers too. Could you help us set up some meetings?"

I have approximately zero authority to say this and neither does Lala, I'm certain. But if we can get people talking, something can be worked out. We can do this—

I notice with a startle that Lala looks gloomy. "I don't know if we can work more closely with the villagers," he says and gestures at himself. "I wouldn't last a day out there without disguising myself. I can only do short trips still." I don't understand. Because he's Jewish, trans, or from the city?

"People won't harass us with me around," Lukrécia adds.

Lala groans. "They're scared to death of the aliens. They just won't show it. You want to gain their trust, that's not the way to go."

The farmers didn't look scared to me, but maybe it was their defense. *Do not show fear.* I'm honestly not sure who's right here, Lala or me, and surely, Lukrécia knows even less than I do to make that decision. Or maybe the villagers were just so afraid for so long that after a while they were too burned out to fear, but they wouldn't not-fear either. I know that kind of empty feeling all too well. Maybe Lala is right after all.

"Right now, we're in three different groups, all isolated, barely interacting," I say. "Villagers, city dwellers, and us alien contact people in Pannonhalma. If we could all work together . . ."

Lala wipes his mouth elaborately with a kerchief and stands. "I'll be off. I have work to do. I'll see if I can send some people your way."

The unspoken message is clear, even to me, even now: don't hold your breath.

"He'll be back shortly," Lukrécia says, back in our room. "Remember, they are observing us."

I look around. There are any number of places to hide something. This was a hotel back in Communist times too. "Are they observing us right now?"

She meows. "I don't have the right sensors to determine that, but I wouldn't be surprised."

My knees are less painful this morning. I chance it. "Let's go for a walk."

The large fountain with the series of ponds is bone-dry, but both the old City Hall building and the Communist-era County Hall across from it are still standing, neo-baroque curlicues mirrored in Modernist glass. This is the center of Győr, and maybe, maybe I can pretend the past twenty years haven't happened. But there are no skaters, no freerunners doing backflips from the stones edging the ponds, and the grass looks more like a vegetable garden than a lawn. Is this where they grow eggplant, I wonder; I know nothing about growing anything. It involves too many sharp objects, and cooking them involves too many hot objects. The best I can do is yank out weeds, but even then, I tend to fall.

I found my niche with the alien contact crowd, and I don't think I'd last here very long. The patience afforded to me both among them and also here is all due to Lukrécia. But Lukrécia speaks fluent, primetime-news Hungarian, so why am I even tagging along? I kick a pebble, and it skitters across cracked paving stones.

I think out loud. "How do we get people to work together? Everyone has isolated themselves, dug in. It would take something really disruptive, like a catastrophe. Back in the day, we could work together when we were facing a common threat."

"There has already been a catastrophe," Lukrécia notes.

"Many years ago. But the balance stabilized. Into something that will just wear us down with time. We'll finish off ourselves, finish what the invaders started." Is it already happening? Mr. Hodász vanishing, the trade slowing . . . everyone growing increasingly weary of the other, even small differences appearing larger and larger . . . the city running out of food . . . the villagers working themselves into utter exhaustion . . . more and more aliens showing up and getting impatient, frustrated, angry . . . who knows when people will start dying again? "I wish Mrs. B. the sociologist was around. I'm sure she'd know the technical terms for this," I tell Lukrécia. "We're forgetting so much." My generation at least got to be teens before the devastation. But what about Lala and the teens his age? We were called Gen Z, but there isn't even a term for his generation.

Pacing is too hard. I sit down on the steps to the fountain.

"Our planet was destroyed," Lukrécia says after a long silence, and I'm not sure if she's trying to one-up me or commiserate. She's my closest confidante, and I don't know her at all.

We walk to the riverside, just a few smoothly curving streets to the north and west. I can still do this. I want to see my favorite spot from way back.

"I will not engineer a disaster," I say to the river. "It would bring people together. But we've all been traumatized enough already." Lukrécia hovers next to me as I wobble down the narrow concrete steps to the water, holding onto the simple railing. The walk is short, but these steps cut into the grassy riverbank are treacherous. Yet I feel compelled to descend, to be closer to the river. I haven't been here for many years. I used to sit on these steps a long time ago, whenever I had a gap in my school schedule and sometimes even when I didn't.

But what else could bring people together if not a disaster? Some other kind of mass event? Could we bring back something like that?

I think of how the townspeople used to march around downtown Győr every year with the relic of Saint Ladislas, singing Catholic hymns. I did it a few times with my family. I knew some of the hymns, even though I wasn't big on church. It was surprisingly uplifting: the singing crowd as it moved along the streets up the hill, down the hill, by the river—a snake made of people, undulating . . .

The Basilica was bombed from orbit, a pinpoint strike.

"Hey, I was looking for you," Lala yells from behind. I turn, barely manage to grab hold of the railing by the steps at the last moment. It holds; after decades of neglect, it still holds. I don't roll down the slope and into the water.

"She hasn't been here in a long time," Lukrécia says. "She's reminiscing."

"I'm thinking about how to bring the three groups together," I say in my best complaining tone, but I'm still shaky after the near fall. My voice wobbles just as much as I do. "I was reminded of the march of Saint Ladislas. I liked that, but that was for Catholics."

He hop-skips down the steps. "What was that?" He has to be Jewish, I think. It's impossible not to know about the march of Saint Ladislas if you're Catholic or even secular. But then he shakes his head and laughs, making a guess why I'm surprised about his ignorance. "I'm from Komárom originally. My parents are still there. I moved here with a caravan two years ago." He shrugs. "Wanted to venture forth. I have no idea what Győr was like before."

To venture forth? He probably wanted to live in a place where fewer people had known him before he transitioned, I think to myself, saying nothing.

Then something clicks into place, and I have to hold on to the railing again. I have an idea. If I can keep myself from falling into the water before saying it.

"Hey, I'll help you up," Lala says, "I don't know how much punishment that rail can take."

I stare at him. "A Pride parade! We could do a Pride parade!"

He laughs. "Have you seen the pictures?"

"What pictures?" I'm perplexed.

We step into the old cinema building that hadn't ever served as a cinema even in my own lifetime. Even before the invasion. I visited maybe once, back when it was used as a concert hall for the Győr Philharmonic. I barely remember how it looked, but it certainly didn't have these wheeled display boards you could pin things on. The kind that were ubiquitous when I was growing up and then never seen again.

It feels like all the lost display boards of the universe have gathered in the lobby. They're mostly filled with drawings pinned to them, but there is the occasional photo, and I wonder who can still make those and how. I vaguely recall something about chemical baths and dark rooms. I step closer.

The drawings are colorful, even rainbowy, and they run the gamut from cheery children's abstraction to more realistic portraits, all with the same bright palette. Some of them show people marching, the backdrops usually barely sketched, but I notice the more recognizable downtown buildings here and there: the Carmelite church, the Turul bird monument on that little square in front of the train station . . . some are portraits of individuals, couples, smaller groups.

The labels glued under the drawings are eerily reminiscent of the sheets I have been filling out. They identify the artist, sometimes also the people in the drawing. There is no "occupation," but there is a line or a paragraph of quotes for everyone: about love, hope, resilience. There are also some sheets entirely covered by quotes, tiny sketches, encouraging messages.

I turn back to Lala grinning at me.

"You've already had a Pride parade," I say.

"Two," he says, shrugging. "We tried. It was an idea to bring people together."

I don't think there were any Pride parades in Győr before the invasion. Maybe someone else also took inspiration from the March of St. Ladislas?

Lala doesn't quite realize how odd all of this is for me. It's like this formerly conservative city turned upside down in my lengthy absence, and I'm here for it.

"I thought I had an original idea." I shrug back.

Lala chuckles. "Well, *we* did not try to involve the aliens . . ."

Lukrécia hovers closer. "Tell me about this idea. I want to know how to bring people together."

This is Lala's moment, and he goes on a long-winded, rambly explanation. Lukrécia makes the occasional encouraging noise, and I keep myself busy looking at the pinboards.

"So what better symbol of hope, uh . . . celebrating our differences," Lala waves his hands, concluding. The dust we stirred up in the lobby twinkles like glitter in the sunlight. "And besides, I know everyone on the organizing committee."

That's great. Not the least because he doesn't seem to know anyone in the town's actual leadership. Though there are such things as formal power and informal power; again, I find myself wishing for Mrs. B. the sociologist. Maybe we can bring her.

I remind myself that if this works out we'll be bringing everyone.

It doesn't take long for Lala to gather the committee in the orchestra hall, find some tables and chairs. I expect the Pride committee members to look outrageously glamorous, but most of them look like they've been dragged away from working on their vegetable patch or hauling salvage. They're more like the crustpunks of yore than David Bowie. Lala tells me there are still a lot of collapsed buildings both farther to the north and also south of the train station. I feel bad; I assumed that, just because the city hall area was preserved, surely everything else must have been too. Even though I knew the Basilica was destroyed.

One of the committee members clears his throat. I can't remember his very ordinary Hungarian men's name. He's a grizzly old man, looks about seventy, which probably means he's around sixty at most. People have just been aging faster with all the hardships; my mind will probably never quite recalibrate to that.

I try to pay attention. I explain haltingly that we all need to work together. They look skeptical, but when I get to the Pride bits, they seem to show more interest. This is their topic.

I get so enthused that I try to push for a march as soon as possible, but a younger woman in a headscarf waves me down. "What you have in mind is a one-time, symbolic event, but you also need to think about the lead-up to it. The preparations are just as important, and the more people get involved, the better."

A young person offers, "People who are skeptical will wait just to see what would happen. They won't cause fuss in the meanwhile."

"Either that, or they'll mobilize to attack the march," the grizzly old man says. I think he must have been to Budapest Pride back in the day.

Lukrécia speaks up. "They won't attack. They're afraid of us."

I bite my tongue. Isn't that the exact impression we are trying to work against here?

People start speaking all at once, and for a moment, I'm sure the meeting will devolve into disorder, but the woman in the headscarf, leading the session, bangs on the table, and everyone falls silent.

Order is restored after that, but as the meeting goes on and on and on, my thoughts drift. I have little more to add, and what I could say, I keep to myself.

I'd rather not mention that I have been wondering if purely physical proximity to the aliens can cause humans to be more understanding. I vaguely recall pheromones from high school biology, before the world crashed on us. But would pheromones work across entirely different physiologies?

Lukrécia is entirely enclosed in a metallic globe, but there are some aliens who can live on Earth unprotected. And some who are experimenting with parasitic relationships with humans. Parasitic? That's not the right word. I search my brain, symbiotic? There was also something else in high school, about how animals eat from a common table . . . commensalism? Mutualism? I'm honestly not sure. There was a chart . . .

Then the meeting gets to the topic of the surrounding villages, and before I manage to refocus, people have already made a decision to organize some kind of county fair instead of the parade.

Instead of?

Combined with, it turns out.

This will be a busy summer season, and for once, I'm glad that the long-term weather has taken a cooler turn with all the dust the invaders kicked up when they bombed us.

III.

Rita M., who turned down the screening, is now staring at me again with all the skepticism she can muster. "A fair. And this is going to help us exactly how? Besides, you said if I put my name down, you won't come back to hassle me."

I shift my weight from one leg to another uncomfortably. Did I walk all the way back here for this? "We're not here to recruit you this time," I tell her. "We're here to help you sell your produce." I try to keep it vague. I know very little about agriculture; I feel like I've been living an isolated life in the alien compound, even with all the recruitment trips.

"At the fair, we'll be able to connect you with wholesale buyers. And it's a one-time event," Lukrécia says.

The girl finally looks at the sphere, tilts her head sideways. "Are *you* interested in eggs?"

"You mean a tractor exhibition?" Bálint P. blinks, rubs his forehead with the back of his hand.

"With a spare-parts market," Lukrécia says.

He turns rapidly to her sphere, and it's as if all the anger's gotten wiped off his face.

"All in one place," I add meekly.

"People would stay here?" Andrea asks, twirling a keyring around her fingers.

I nod. "We were thinking of using the old campground as the fairgrounds . . .? By the foot of the hill? And people could stay in your cabins up the hill?"

"I'm sure you'd run the inn at full capacity for the duration of the fair," Lukrécia offers. "And some of those visitors might be interested in coming back later too."

We stay in one of the old kids' cabins overnight. It's a big ask to use the grounds, so we might as well give the inn a bit more business in the meanwhile.

By the time I finally get to bed, I ache all over. So much walking! I wish I had enough balance to ride a bike, but the roads are in such bad shape, it might be pointless anyway. And there's no reason to go all the way back to Győr before we talk to the aliens.

I startle, and my legs twitch.

Lukrécia hovers closer. "What happened?"

"I was just thinking about everything while falling asleep. And I realized, when I was thinking of *we*, I was thinking of you and me . . ." I'm probably too sleepy to explain anything. "I don't think we are aliens. To each other. Anymore." I turn toward her, even though my whole body protests, and my arms get tangled in the fluffy blanket. "I mean, we've been friends. For a while. But. I just instinctively thought of you as . . . like me. Like here are *us*, and there are the *aliens*."

"I assume that's good," Lukrécia says, ever so patient. "I do believe you should sleep though."

I fall asleep to her slow purring.

At the compound, we meet Mrs. B. before anyone else; she comes up to us, her face glowing with eagerness. "The two of you gave me my life back," she says. "Finally, something meaningful to do!"

I'm quite sure that fixing machinery and keeping chickens is also meaningful, but I don't feel up to a debate with her. I vaguely nod, and she takes this as encouragement.

"I immediately noticed that our problem was organization, or rather the lack thereof," she waves toward the base. "There are many projects, but they are not coordinated. People hide the lack of organization with forceful demands." I nod, thinking of the quotas I've always felt were impossible to fill. She goes on: "So I designed a communication needs survey and administered it to everyone with the aid of the nice young people here. When we could not communicate with certain individuals at all, we noted that. Then we could identify areas of immediate need . . ."

We walk inside. She provides me with the verbal equivalent of a wall of text, and I like listening to her. I get the impression she's neuroatypical like me, just in a different way. Is she autistic? Does she have ADHD? She probably knows all the terms for everything, but that would be a different wall of text. Maybe we can do that next time.

"How much do you know about folklore?" she asks me abruptly.

"Uh, why?" I feel like all I know about folklore I learned from video games back when we still had them.

"There is one group with a device that they cannot operate. It's not a translator per se. The closest we got was some kind of 'telepathy machine,' but I'm questioning the use of the term. Their communications officer died in transit, and now, they're looking for someone similar to use the device. They told me to find them a *witch*!" She laughs. "So just in case this isn't *another* mistranslation, I was wondering if you could find me a witch."

I'm not surprised by anything at this point. "I'm sure there'll be plenty of opportunity for that at the fair," I tell her.

"What fair?" She looks apprehensive at first, but in under ten minutes, she becomes our biggest advocate.

The riverside by the Carmelite church in Győr is calm and quiet. Save for Lala, Lukrécia, and me.

"We convinced the city leadership," Lala says, talking animatedly and pacing on the concrete-block fence on top of the floodbank. "I felt the arguments were a bit on the utilitarian side, but hey, everyone likes fresh produce." He makes a face. "So if your people are in, my people are in."

I nod at him cheerfully from below. If I tried to get up there, I'd fall. "Remember I was telling you about the elderly sociologist lady? We ran into her again, and it turned out she'd made friends with literally all the aliens in just a few days. They loved her. She thought that the fair and parade would be a great idea, so all of a sudden, everyone was on board." I chuckle. "Now we only need to find her a witch."

Lala blinks, bursts out in laughter, and hops down. "A witch?"

I explain, with big, sweeping gestures. I even lose track of my utter exhaustion for a while.

Lala scratches his head. "Sanyi is handy with a dowsing rod. Would that count?"

I stare at him in bafflement. He turns apologetic. "We don't have the old utility maps. Do you have any idea how hard it is to dig downtown without hitting a pipe?"

I'm shocked. "But that's like . . . superstition. Pseudoscience?"

Lala giggles. "He's still pretty handy with it though!"

I figure Mrs. B. can run a controlled research trial. My job is just to get people to talk to each other.

IV.

I imagined something organized and tidy, something beautiful that emerges from the collaboration of thousands of different people.

What emerges from the collaboration of thousands of different people is a giant mess.

Many of the aliens grasp the concept of a parade but clearly don't understand about floats. A giant snake slithers on top of Bálint's tractor, which has been decorated with ribbons like a maypole, and then crushes the entire vehicle. Bálint starts to weep. Witchy Sanyi turns out to be one of the grizzled crustpunks from the city council, and the impatient aliens have him try the machine right then and there, in the middle of the crowd, which results in him projecting his emotions over a twenty-meter radius. He is apparently very hungry. The people near him mob Rita's family stall, which sells corn-on-the-cob, and topple it over. A chicken brought for display escapes until it is caught by a many-tentacled and triangular alien, who has some kind of dramatic reaction to it. Body fluids are involved, and people yelling, "Let me through. I'm a doctor," but the alien waves them away with three tentacles on three sides. I wonder if I'll ever find Mr. Hodász. He could be making a killing in trade at the fair, but he doesn't seem to be here, according to every farmer I asked. I wonder if you can find people with a dowsing rod, and I make a mental note to ask Sanyi or Mrs. B. about this later; once they have both eaten their fill of corn.

I wasn't very closely involved with the organizing in the final stages, so now I try to relax and move with the erratic, sputtering flow. I walk through the entrance, under a gorgeously elaborate sign saying "THE 1st INTERSPECIES SOLIDARITY FAIR AND PARADE." It sways as people of various species bump against the entryway. Someone is carrying a bunch of signs clearly repurposed from the Pride parade and gets tangled in a clutch of kids' balloons. I haven't seen balloons in at least a decade, but someone must have been stockpiling them. I thought they wouldn't last so long, but maybe there is a way to store them . . . or were the aliens printing them on one of their ships? I can't even think of that conversation. How do you explain "balloon" when you can barely communicate about your immediate needs?

"I thought an *apocalypse* would finally get us to give up *plastic*," someone my age and in a sparkly dress grumbles next to me. I shrug apologetically. I'm looking around for Lala. I spot him with a very tall person handing out signs. Lala gets one saying "FAITH, HOPE, CHARITY" in rainbow letters above what looks like a very complicated version of the trans symbol.

I remember *that* slogan from somewhere; for a moment, I feel something go crosswired in my brain as I dredge up the right memory from an age gone by. "The three Catholic virtues, huh?" I nod at him, half-yelling in the noise. The unknown sign-maker must have been missing the march of St. Ladislas.

He looks at the sign in puzzlement. "Are they?" He glances around, but the person has already been carried away by the crowd. "You know I'm Jewish, right?" he yells back.

I shrug. "I guessed. Here, I'll take it." Not that I should be carrying a large sign. It looks like a recipe for injuring others.

"Are you Catholic?" he asks.

"I was baptized . . ."

He shrugs too. "I was also baptized." He chuckles at my confusion. "My great-grandma said you needed to have the right documents."

"Even in an apocalypse?" I look around. A cream-colored butterfly lands on my shoulder, and then another.

"Especially in an apocalypse."

But we don't get to think about the grim moments of Hungarian history because a large metallic sphere rolls past—the size of Lukrécia's but with a brass tint. It's very much not floating or doing anything that it's supposed to do. And it's being chased by a Chasid and an Austrian farmer who are yelling at each other in what sounds like the same language, be it Lower Austrian German or Yiddish. They finally catch the sphere and steady it. They pat it and rumble at it in an oddly parental way. How do you say, "It's going to be all right," in Yiddish? I suppose exactly like that.

We stare, stunned, until Lukrécia floats calmly next to us, saying, "I was wondering if that 'first' on the sign above the entrance was a promise or a threat."

"I don't think anyone's going to forget this day anytime soon," Lala nods at her. He's smiling, and he looks more relaxed than ever before, despite all the chaos and noise.

"Isn't that the kind of thing that's supposed to bring people together—shared memories? Or commiseration?" I try to ask, but my voice is drowned out, first by the collapsing gate and then by the buzzing of three flying aliens, trying to keep the pieces from tumbling into the crowd. I shiver; how lucky that they were in the right place at the right time . . .

"If we make it through all this without anyone getting injured, that will be a miracle in itself," I tell Lukrécia once the gate is safely dismantled.

"Fret not," Mrs. B. says from behind me. "My precognitive squad is doing double duty."

"That didn't save Bálint's beloved tractor," I grumble at her because it's still easier to be grouchy than to be astonished. Even if my anger is dissipating.

"We'll get him a new one," Mrs. B. says, biting into a cob, and I don't need to ask her who is *we*.

It is us, all of *us*, from now on.

A TECHNICAL TERM, LIKE PRIVILEGE

GET HOME AND THE RENTAL NEEDS TO DRINK MY BLOOD. AGAIN, ALWAYS, the fourth time this week and it's only Wednesday. I strip off my top, undershirt. I'm not going to take off my pants, I don't care what the rental thinks. Does it think?

I think it only feels, feels a deep resentment of humans living inside its caverns, its air bubbles. Housebeasts have sensory nerve endings on the inside, feel us tickling them as we live our petty lives, squeeze us for blood.

The life of flesh is in the blood, the preachers say. The housebeast doesn't need my blood, type O, good for transfusions. It needs the magic. But most people, their magic is sparse, less heavily invested in their body. The housebeast needs the blood, to squeeze out every drip of sustenance—not from the blood itself but from what it carries.

While tentacles slither around on my skin, while the wall glues itself to me, I wonder for the fifth time what I can do to get out of this. I feel my bone marrow straining to produce more red blood cells. I need a break. The wall grabs a lock of hair, and I know it's a total loss—I'll have to cut that one off too. Should've just worn a cap, should've cut it all short—should, should. I need to call the rental office.

Twelve apartments in this beast, or was it fourteen? The third beast on the block, a student neighborhood. It was all right before the semester started. I don't know what the new students are doing, but the beast needs so much more magic now. Are people puking in the disposal-holes? Trying to squeeze out broadband from the beast-nerves?

The worst part of it is, it feels good while the beast drinks. It needs me, yes, but I can feel that it loves me. It wants to keep me close.

I stagger away from the wall, rubbing my bruised skin, crashing onto the sofa, staining the cover. Too tired to take a shower, but at least we'll have enough water pressure now. My hand is searching for the receiver, and it helpfully pops out, shakes drips—of what, synovial fluid?—off of itself. I groan into the receiver, ask for the rental office.

"Yes, I understand it needs the magic. Yes, I understand these were the terms when I signed. I was"—I take a heavy breath—"just wondering if it needs to be so . . . direct. I mean, I can give it magic without the blood. I can do that."

I scratch the side of the receiver with a stubby fingernail. It squirms. I'm too faint to understand the explanation from the chirpy person on the other end of the line in an office somewhere nearer the head. But it's a no—it's always a no. "The contracts aren't written with someone like you in mind, you have to understand," but heck, they need me if they want to keep the beast going. Maybe they should recruit from the Department of Applied Magic and not from, I don't know, engineering students.

Then again, I didn't go into magic either. That shit is for the highborn.

I fall asleep, wake a few hours later. I am late with my homework in Entirely Useless Studies, but I can't muster the enthusiasm. A graduate degree, yes. Your fellowship will pay your tuition, yes. But all the money I get from teaching on the side goes into renting this room that I couldn't even call a cavern. And the food, the iron supplements lately, those cheap industrial hotdogs pushed out by a factorybeast. I hear some of the highborn mages are vegetarian, and I wonder how they swing it. I need to get another twelve-pack of eggs, low-cost protein. I wonder if I could raise chickens without the rental office noticing. Is chicken feed cheaper than eggs? Chickens smell though. I wonder how long I'd last before I roasted them on a spit—live for today, don't mind tomorrow.

By the heavens, I'm hungry. I rub my face, but that doesn't summon food. I find my last hotdog in the cooling pouch. I eat it cold, can't wait out the minute to warm it up. I need to shower. I need to go. I saw this flyer on campus, and maybe it can be just the thing.

I run my fingers along the words. I feel scrubbed. The hot water was great in the shower—never mind it took my blood and sweat to boil it.

ONWARD TO ARMS! FOR THE REVOLUTION!

The Communards of Szederkei County invite YOU to our Campus Meetings . . .

The address is off campus but close by. Some university official probably ousted them. No one wants to deal with a bunch of rabble-rousers, well, except the rabble-rousers like me. I crunch the leaflet back into the pocket of my robe.

Two tall, pale dudes are by the door, and I feel acutely scrawny. Possibly also insufficiently cis. But that's not what they complain about. At least, I *think* it's not that, though one never knows really.

One of them fingers my pendant, and I flinch from the touch. I had too much touch today already, even if not the human kind.

They say something about no mages—and I can't quite make it out, I'm worse off than I'd thought—and I get into a debate with them. One of them just keeps on repeating that mages are a privileged class. As if that was some technical term, and for all I know, it is.

"You can do something other people can't. That's a privilege."

I can't even muster a glare. I feel like I can't do anything because I've been sucked dry of every last drop of blood. And I can't argue well either because what, I mean, he's technically right. I can do things other people can't.

I walk away wordless, but a debate rages in my head. All the highborn mages, that's privilege. But why can't I. I mean I can. Maybe it's just that I'm a failure. I wanted to pick myself up by my bootstraps, get a fellowship, study Useless Studies—I mean mathematics. (I actually love it. When I can keep my eyes straight to stare at a page.) Get into fights with engineering students, grow up, get into grad school, stop getting into fights. Moan about engineering students and how they vomit into every available receptacle after a night of drinking and more fights. All while I need to make sure the housebeast has enough energy to digest all that crap. I'm sure I did the same as a first-year, but that was before the rental hikes, before grad students got pushed out of on-campus housing.

I was better at fights, to be honest. Still not late for a career as a cage fighter maybe, but I value my brain cells, and I can't afford the protective enchantments.

Rika stares at me over their bagged lunch: a sandwich of what, bread and cheese probably. They're looking tired today, colorful hair hidden in a hastily wrapped scarf, their skin patchy pink. "Stop thinking about witty repartee," they say.

I shake my head. I've been thinking of so many rejoinders. I could've yelled at those people that I was trans, but if they didn't guess, wasn't that also *privilege*? What if they did guess? It wasn't like I could quiz them. "How did you know?" I ask Rika.

"It's all over your face," they chuckle, their voice dry. "Staircase wit, it's called. You come up with it when you're already walking down the stairs."

"Well yeah, other buildings have staircases. Mine has an esophagus."

"You could unionize." They just toss that out there as if that was so easy.

"What, a renters' union?" I'm laughing.

"Exactly that." They're frustrated with me, I can feel. Their mind vibrates. They put down the sandwich and lean forward. "I'm not studying sociology because it's so good. I'm studying it because I want to beat them at their game."

A blanket *them* that can cover everyone. From greedy landlords to Revolutionary Communards.

I shake my head. "I couldn't even get into a proper resistance meeting."

"Eat something. You'll feel better." They tilt their head. "Want one of my sandwiches?"

"What's inside?"

"Um, bread and cheese?"

I take it.

At home again, my turn to squeeze broadband out of the nerves. I read and read, and all I conclude is that everyone has their own jargon, subversives included. I feel resentment toward *the apparatus of revolution*. I'm not the right kind of comrade, and I feel I can't even complain.

Even if I could find a new place mid-semester, which I couldn't knowing my luck, who's to say it won't go exactly the same? I used to live on Butchers Row in the inorganic housing before it got demolished, and at one point, the floor cracked open, and I found myself knee-deep in my downstairs neighbor's ceiling just like that. Another housebeast, and that'll probably go the same. Every place that has an opening this time of the year will probably be salivating for magic. The beast or the owners, I wonder.

Am I the only one in this situation? I don't know, but I guess everyone else who might be is probably likewise flattened out from all the blood loss.

I glare at the dark-purple walls, the rugged, ribbed interior of the housebeast. Why does it need me? I can't even hate it. I feel bad for it. It's trapped same as I am. It needs my cheap blood, filled with magic and whatever power comes out of a hotdog after it's digested. I'm surprised my terrible diet hasn't poisoned it already.

Well, that would certainly be a way to take revenge on the rental office. Or just to make the argument again that I could be doing this without the blood. Maybe that would convince them.

I half cough, half guffaw. Instead of pamphlets, I could be reading about the biochemistry of housebeasts.

It takes effort to find out which substances can accumulate in my blood with less harmful effect to me than to the housebeast. Everything takes effort when I'm so woozy, lying on the sofa, scratching my still-churning belly. Exhaustion can look a lot like laziness, and I only hope an idle rental clerk isn't looking in on me via the beast's internal photosensor cells. It can be done.

I hope I'm not interesting enough.

It takes even more effort to find a substance I can easily add to my diet. I've never stolen food, and maybe it's not the best to begin when I'm keeling over from anemia and a distinct lack of magic. I budget and rebudget. The numbers don't add up. Maybe Rika has a thunderfruit tree in their back yard. Maybe I can find a restaurant that gets rid of a few pounds of a very specific mushroom every day. Maybe, maybe. I could use my magic for this if I had any left over after feeding the beast. As if.

I feel like dirt for even contemplating harming a living creature, but I can't keep up this feeding schedule. It's not about hurting an animal for fun. It's about bare survival. Would I slaughter a cow to eat it? Oh yes, I would. I'm an inveterate city dweller, but I'd give it an honest try if the need was pressing. Is this so different?

I scribble numbers on my slate. I look at an Intro to Pharmacokinetics text. I make guesses about my metabolism. Fuck if I know how magic affects all this.

Two full measures of thunderfruit a day while minimizing other liquid intake. That shouldn't be so hard. In just a few days, this will cause striking cutaneous symptoms on both interior and exterior membranes. Of the housebeast, not of me. Worst case, I might get a mild rash. Diarrhea from all the thunderfruit.

If I time it well, skin will slough from the ceiling straight into people's breakfasts. I wonder if I can adjust it so that it happens in the offices near the head first, where the rental company is safely cocooned.

Public databases are a close second to magic. Here are all the public trees on city plots. All the fruit-bearing trees. All the thunderfruit trees. Here, watch me draw a path connecting them all. If I take one from each, I'll have two full measures per day easy, and no one will notice. You're not supposed to harvest them, but you can take for personal use.

My personal use is just a little more demanding is all.

Here is the path. Only three Imperial miles on foot. Per day. While my bone marrow cries in agony as it grinds away at producing new blood cells.

All my limbs hurt. By the second day, I know I'll have to involve somebody.

I explain my plan to Rika, sitting in the park at a chessboard, pretending to play. I connect imaginary dots.

"Once they realize my blood is useless for the beast, they'll surely allow me to give my magic without giving blood. I just have trouble getting enough thunderfruit."

They shake their head. "What's to say they won't just boot you from the rental?"

A sudden pounding ache in my stomach. I can feel my magic going askew. I must *believe* in my plan, but Rika . . . Rika is so sensible. They're probably right.

"Believe me," I say, but I can't believe myself anymore.

I'll just have to stop talking to Rika. Stop talking to anyone. *I will be my own internal revolution,* I think to myself as I mash the thunderfruit together in a bowl, shovel it into my mouth. It is gooey sweet and just vaguely medicinal, that kind of pharmacy aftertaste.

Two measures of thunderfruit a day is an awful lot. Bodybuilders do this with rice and what, chicken? I'll think of this as my spiritual discipline. I should believe in the kindly powers, but the kindly powers had never so much glanced at me; they stranded me with enough magic to be sucked dry but not enough standing to become a mage. Not the right family, not the right gender, not the right anything. What is the right gender even.

The housebeast skips a day with its requests, and another. Is it suspecting something?

My blood stews. Then my guts churn. I didn't think about this—will my excrement poison the beast even faster? I considered everything so carefully. How did I miss this? I should've gone into Useful Studies, like medicine.

I drag myself to the academy and lock myself into one of the restrooms there, near the Department of Complex Systems where no one ever goes anyway. I think wistfully of my research projects, now abandoned. I am my own project.

There is a sticker in the toilet stall, telling me where to look for help with domestic violence. There is no sticker about being eaten alive by your rental. I still wonder about reaching out. Does this count? Surely there has to be a limit to how much blood can be extracted from a person on a regular basis. My contract only specified something vague based on "needs and capabilities." It's just my luck that I'm probably the most magical person in this particular housebeast. It's like not having enough bandwidth because there is only one outgoing nerve bundle for the whole floor.

I stumble against the door when I try to exit the stall. I'm not one for religion, but even I think about invoking the kindly powers.

Rika has left a message while I was gone, and I ignore it. I can't risk being discouraged.

As I topple on the sofa, I feel a pang that's something new, not my upset stomach or my head foggy from blood loss. I feel a need, and I'm not sure if it's the beast's or mine. It feels good, being fed on, after all. And for three days, I've gone without.

I laugh bitterly. The housebeast beckons.

This is the time. Breakfasts and convoluted schedules are irrelevant. Now is the time.

May the kindly powers help me. Help us all.

I peel off my shirt, tearing a strap in the process. I fumble with my undershirt, sprain a finger that I hooked under it just wrong. I laugh-cry. I lean against the wall, and the wall leans against me, tentacles reaching out. Even my own smell feels different. Has the change in my metabolism been so drastic already?

The housebeast drinks deeply and pauses for a moment—

It retches the blood out in a spasming stream onto my floor and my half-full, half-empty backpack.

I sit on the floor, a familiar numb shock, and time passes and passes and passes until someone from the rental office comes by to draw my blood, test it. I offer my arm without words.

"You have a week to make sure your numbers are within range and your blood passes the filter," the clerk says chirpily, her hair arcing straight around her face as she tosses her head to the side. "Otherwise, your contract will be terminated at the end of the week."

My mouth moves finally, slowly. "How am I supposed to find a place mid-semester?"

Filters. I didn't think the beast would have filters. What do they filter out?

The clerk says something that's not even apologetic.

"Can I give. My magic. Without the blood. I can do it. Just look at my results," I croak and beg.

I don't understand the answer beyond the *no*.

"Can I please. I promise I can do it." I raise my voice.

"You need to stop threatening me," the clerk says.

I'm small and half-covered in my own blood and feeling like I'm about to die. *I'm not* threatening *you*, I think—but I don't say anything. She's read me as male, I know. As someone potentially threatening. I don't want to give the company yet another reason to boot me from the rental.

She is going on about how they're going to make sure it'll all go on my record.

Something about the police. Something about one last chance to get my act together and stop drinking that filth that passes for alcohol in the alleys near the academy. One week. Or she'll make sure—*you have to understand it's not about your person*—that my "violent behavior" gets reported.

That wouldn't put an end to finding a room. It'd put an end to my studies, to everything I've scraped together all this miserable life.

I want to pace the room, but I can't. Mopping up the blood has used up all the energy I had left. I lie on the floor, convinced there's still a puddle underneath me, but I can't.

Why do they need my blood?

"The kindly powers have saved you from me," I tell the housebeast and chuckle. "They've saved you, not me." My abdominal muscles spasm from my attempt to laugh. Speaking is hard. I can just think at the beast—we are connected well enough at this point.

I don't want to hurt you, I think. *But I can't keep this up.*

The beast is so hungry.

You're in a bad situation too, huh? I turn to my side, fetal position. Even my thoughts are hard to sustain. *In a reasonable world, the rental company would just hire some mages to deal with the shortfall.*

What is it that my blood does that my magic can't?

Rika finds me on the floor, and I'm muttering the same question to them.

They always take me seriously. They answer, talking to me while they're sponging me down, feeding me with something refreshingly solid. Rice cakes?

"Giving your blood ensures you don't have enough energy left to rebel," they say. "You have more than enough magic to cause a mess."

That's certainly possible. I nod.

"And also . . ." They fall silent, bite their lower lip. "Divide and conquer. If you can be kept away from other people fighting for equality, so much the better for the people in power."

I blink at them.

"Don't tell me you bought into this bullshit take on class struggle." They glare at me. "I'll be blunt with you. Magic doesn't make you into an aristocrat."

"I still pass as male," I say weakly.

"Look, take this from one trans person to another, all right? You don't pass anywhere near consistently, I'm sorry. And do you even want to? I mean, you're not a man exactly."

I groan. "My gender is a mess."

They wave at me. "Your gender is just fine. You just need some stability in your life. Look, you're trying to convince me how privileged you are just as you are in the process of being slowly eaten alive. Can you have some compassion for yourself?"

I will not cry. Am I crying? "I tried to hurt the housebeast."

"That's the same thing. You think of the housebeast as your opponent, not as your comrade."

"It is trying to eat me . . .?"

"It's hungry because it's been deprived of resources. That's my best sociological analysis really."

I stand up, immediately dizzy, and sit back down. Rika is right. Terribly, terribly right. "Why are you helping me?" That's not what I want to say.

"You helped me out back in first year, and now I'm helping you out." They pause. "But to be honest, I'm just telling you this so that you can feel satisfied. I know that for you it's all give and take. But sometimes I just want to help out my friends. I can't stand to see you all alone, working yourself into a small desperate corner."

I try to protest, but Rika is still right. They don't have much magic, but their thoughts move along such orderly lines that they pull my own thoughts along.

After Rika leaves, I lay down to sleep, but it's as if some kind of barrier had tumbled down inside me, and instead of dreams, I join—join the housebeast.

The housebeast is hungry and sad and disappointed and frustrated and hungry and disappointed. Heck, now *I'm* hungry.

The housebeast has an immediate response to run away, to fly—

Hold on, I think at the housebeast, at myself, *running away would solve precisely nothing. Where would we go? What about your other inhabitants?*

I am treated to a plan of all the inhabitants' movements, a time-lapse, points of minimal and maximal activity—

You've thought about this, have you?

Was *I* keeping the housebeast from running away? I was a prime source of sustenance. But I could send magic remotely if with some additional difficulty . . .

That's why it had to be blood. If people were allowed to feed housebeasts with pure magic without a carrying substrate, anyone could go anywhere. Housebeasts could go anywhere. Broke grad students could go anywhere. Societal control would be loosened.

I'm starting to think like Rika.

I can feed you without the blood, I think at the housebeast, *if that works for you.* My magic replenishes faster than my red blood cells at least. *We won't have to tell anyone. We'll just pretend.*

The housebeast doesn't quite understand *pretend* and is hungry, so hungry.

We can sort it out. I shrug, my shoulders shot through with pain at the motion, my awareness abruptly recentered on my body. I have just eaten—my last hotdogs if memory serves. I can do this. I tell the housebeast, *You can feed.*

Do I sleep, or do I just blink off, I don't even.

I know when I wake that something is askew. I drag myself to my feet, and the floor tilts. I fall. My left ankle cracks. The startle blanks out the pain. I don't have a window—windows are only on higher levels—where's the door? I'm in some random shirt and underwear and naked legs, and it shows how bad the situation has gotten. I can't be bothered about the legs. I half walk, half topple out the door, and it opens with the usual smacking sound, but there are some weird harmonics in it that I can't quite tease out.

I crash into the rental clerk with the fancy hair. We all have our ways of trying to hold on to something that makes us feel human, I suppose. I understand her all too well for a moment, and I wonder if I have too much magic left, if that can even be a thing.

"The anchors have detached," she says. "All shards have failed." And this has to be a technical term too, like *privilege*.

I feel ridiculous. What did Rika say, something about revolution being structural change that cannot be achieved by any one individual's heroic actions, something something? This is bad. Is the housebeast flying? The housebeast's flying after taking enough power from me to tear off the anchors and rise to the skies. So now we'll probably get shot down with anti-air cannons for all I know. My one-person rebellion—how privileged. How pointless.

"I've let it loose," I mutter. "Sorry, I didn't mean to." But truly, did I?

The clerk stares at me, and no, I can't make out her thoughts. The floor wobbles and I feel a pull, a pull at my guts, or at least something somewhere inside me—

"You fainted," the rental clerk says. Am I on the floor? I must be. She's somewhere out of arm's reach. It makes sense. She doesn't dare to be closer to me.

"No one's thinking about anything," I tell her, and in my head, this makes sense too. The beast didn't think this through—a characteristic of beasts of all sorts. I didn't think this through.

Even without the blood, the beast will fly and drain me and drain and . . .

"Almost everyone is out at this hour," she says. "So I figured it had to be you. Of course."

"Structural change," I say with brutal effort, fighting my mouth gone rubbery numb. "We need to descend. Do you know how to steer?"

"Steer what? They are supposed to be anchored—"

Rika would surely have an amazing idea. There is no plan, nothing, just my need to get away from it all that the housebeast has clearly internalized. A big, giant cursing that fills the skies. The kind of pointless anger that makes the rental clerk flinch away from me as I stagger to my feet. I still don't know her name, but I can't move and speak at the same time, and something's got to go.

The beast didn't digest the poison, but something made it through the filters after all. Something that's grimy and base as only emotion can get.

I'll hate myself in the afterlife, surrounded by the kindly powers gently but insistently telling me off.

I only know this, am only driven by this—I need to at least see for myself what's happening before we all pancake on the ground.

The front gate is so far. It opens, opens, and I'm stunned. I expect the rushing air, but there's some kind of giant flap that had extruded out of the wall, and it's keeping the worst of the impact off me.

Also, we are close to the ground. Uncomfortably close. Tears the snot out of my nose close.

Are we right above Rika's housebeast?

I brace for impact. The clerk at my right loudly prays.

Down just below, I see the other housebeast's front gate open, and I cuss.

Rika looks up at me, our eyes lock across the distance like they shouldn't, and Rika's incredulity makes it across whatever connection we have built, mind to mind.

Their beast wobbles. Moorings detaching? Rika ducks back inside. Are they whooping? They must be. I'm not sure how I can tell through the noise, must be the magic. Their beast is eager to join mine. Something draws them together. Pheromones or possibility? Magic, physics, wait maybe that newfound social context—so hilarious as to feel plausible. Wrenching really. The beast breaks loose from the ground with a crack I feel in my teeth.

"This structural enough for you?" I scream at the top of my lungs, and I laugh, laugh as my housebeast swings low and up again on a neat parabola as Rika's housebeast gains speed and altitude as all around us the masses of cheap rentals detach from the ground, take to the air.

Every jug of water has that one last drop before it overflows, I find myself thinking. The conditions were here: the hungry beasts, the grip of control loosening its hold. I'm just one person, and the heroic deeds are for another, but out of the mess, this emerged, and maybe others can make sense of it.

The ocean's near, so near, and all I can hope for is that when I pass out, we'll be above water and maybe, just maybe, free once and for all.

POWER TO YIELD

in memory of A

0.

OYĀRUN CLOSED HER EYES TO CONCENTRATE ON THE VIDEO SHE WAS viewing through her neural interface. She wanted to finish her civics homework assignment fast. Just a few more hours, and then she would be done with everything that wasn't on the pre-engineering track. She could get back to what actually interested her, lose herself in that . . .

Not now, she wrenched her thoughts back to her assignment. The attention shift was almost painful.

Pick a high-importance political event in recent history. List three major stakeholders, and present their viewpoints with special attention to conflicts. It sounded hard. She was a math person, not even sure where to begin. She picked this event because it had happened shortly after Independence.

The recording was three-dimensional but relatively low resolution. Oyārun watched, trying to recall some context that she could use for the assignment. At the time of the recording, beat-up space transports carrying refugees from the Empire were still streaming to the small planetoid of Eren, and a vote had just been passed to increase ambient gravity in living areas. People were still hammering out the political details of the new state; the High Council was yet unformed, existing only as an informal social conglomerate of like-minded leaders.

These leaders were standing at a podium, surrounded by a vast crowd. Oyārun only recognized some of them from her previous studies, and the person now moving toward the front to speak was unfamiliar to her.

She pulled up the annotations for the video, cross-referenced them with the Eren-wide social network. *Aramīn, also known as Armyn, formerly of the Imperial House of Gubhas on the High Plains of Emek. Male, living alone, not interested in—*she shooed away the panel. It was helpful to know he was still alive. He wasn't in his elder years yet, but people had died in all sorts of accidents in the early days. She wasn't interested in his personal circumstances beyond that. Something clicked: wasn't he one of the very few Imperial nobles who'd supported independence?

Aramīn looked mixed, Imperial and Plainsfolk, possibly also Northerner. She couldn't make out the details of his face beyond the pale skin and long black hair, carefully braided with thinner braids joining into three larger ones, hanging well past his shoulders on both sides, and—she'd seen when he turned around—also along his back. A symbol of nobility. The video did not allow her to zoom in further, and she resisted requesting an interpolation; she could pull up his profile again later.

She missed the first few sentences.

"Denounce oppression. Denounce subjugation. And take a firm stand." The crowd seemed restless, murmuring, pulling at their scarves, scratching their heads under their caps. Aramīn went on, speaking firmly and loudly, his voice carrying even past the amplification. "Imperial Seers were subjugated and forced to labor for the Court, the very same Court that declared a major cognotype to be Undesirable, its bearers to be eradicated from the gene pool. The same attitude undergirds both: a greediness to prescribe value. A greediness to be the only source of truth and justice. A greed."

The crowd was quieting down. Paying attention? Oyārun leaned forward, even though that wouldn't help her see better. She was intrigued.

"We are all here together now. Undesirables and Seers, from all peoples of the Empire of the Three Stars, the Empire of Emek: Imperials, Worowans,

Northerners, Plainsfolk, and more. And the people who have stood with Undesirables and Seers in solidarity."

Aramīn paused. Took a deep breath.

"You all know that I am neither a Seer nor an Undesirable. Yet I chose to stand by the cause of independence. I am Armyn, formerly the head of a noble house and currently head of the High Plains Research Institute. A surgeon, a medical scientist. I come from a high position. And more—I supplied young Seers for the noble houses. I trained them and let them be eaten alive by the insatiable hunger of the Court, always desperate for more magic, until those young Seers said no more. Until I said no more. Until we said no more. They rose up, and I rose up. They spoke, and I listened."

A chill ran along Oyārun's spine. Aramīn spoke in an even tone, but he was brutally direct. People wouldn't speak of the war in such a straightforward way anymore. He went on, not backing down: "I cannot claim to know what it is like to be a Seer. I never had to wear Seer's robes. I never had my head shaved, treated with a poison so that my hair would never grow out again, so that I would stand out in a crowd, so that I would not be able to escape, would not be able to hide.

"But now we stand all together. On this land, this planetoid deemed uninhabitable by the Empire, we are equal."

Oyārun watched, entirely breathless, not even daring to fidget for fear that the magic of the moment would pass. Aramīn went on.

"Yet whenever you look at me, you see me—and you see a symbol of Imperial might. You see my hair past my shoulders. You see a man who was never tortured. And you remember your pain." His voice lifted higher and higher, working itself into a crescendo. "I say we are equal, and my actions shall mirror my words. We shall all be equal, and I am willing to take the first step. We are not just Seer and not just Undesirable and not just anyone else. We are all this and more. We are a people—a people arising from murder and bloodshed, a people arising from genocide, a people who have fought hard for our freedom." He dropped his voice abruptly, continuing in a quiet, calm tone: "And I shall be just like anyone else."

Aramīn raised a hand, a blade glinting into the camera for a moment. He cut off his thick braids, one by one, with motions that seemed impossibly practiced. With an economy of gesture. He turned to one of his fellow councilpeople, someone Oyārun recognized: Esokaruwe, a former Imperial Seer and a leader of resistance fighters. A fearsome warrior.

"Esteemed Esokaruwe, if you please." He handed the blade to her. Esokaruwe seemed stunned, but began to cut his hair, confused, hands moving slowly, jaggedly. Oyārun thought she must not have been privy to Aramīn's plan.

It took a while. Esokaruwe steeled herself, tensed her muscles as she worked, hacking away at the remaining hair, shaving Aramīn's scalp. Then Aramīn turned to her and said something in an undertone, too quiet for the camera to pick up. She gestured for him to turn around and passed her hands slowly over his scalp. Oyārun could not sense it through the recording, but she knew that Esokaruwe was using the māwal to scour Aramīn's head. He would not grow hair again. Oyārun ran a hand along her own hairless scalp in an attempt to ground herself in physical reality. But she wouldn't pause the recording. She had to see it all for herself.

The other councilpeople who hadn't been Seers were already lining up, dazed and shocked, milling in place. Limbs twitched as they waited for their turn. Aramīn had *not* run this by them, Oyārun thought. But she knew this had been the moment when Ereni became Ereni; from the disparate groups of Seers and Undesirables and whoever else had escaped to the planetoid with them, one united people began forming at this very instant. Blades flashed here and there among the crowd, and slowly, people removed their head coverings. Some were bald former Seers, stunned by the sudden turn of events, wrenched out of their course that even their precognition had not foreseen. Others were Undesirables of various ethnicities, uncomfortable but willing to join the Seers. Cutting their hair in silence, only the low murmurs of people asking each other for help. Making a point of solidarity. With all the weapons in the crowd, there was not a moment of violence. Oyārun watched, breathless, until the video finished.

It had to happen. Oyārun had read a lot about the tensions between the two groups, threatening to drive apart the newly founded Free State of Eren. But she'd never before realized that it was someone who was neither a Seer nor an Undesirable who'd forced the issue.

An Imperial noble who felt entitled enough to do so.

Who shaped history.

This was not the history Oyārun had been taught. And she needed, desperately needed, to know more.

I.

1.

> *Aramīn is ... people will say he's a sadist and a Falconer, I know. And*
> *I suppose some of that is true. But he's also a brilliant surgeon, and a*
> *researcher, and ... [P: 0.8v] Not what you expect from a noble. We all ...*
> *[P: 0.5v] [to say] liked him might be too strong ... [but] we appreciated him,*
> *certainly. All the folk up in HPR.*
>
> —Amasewun ta Yowasiru, Ereni Oral History Archives,
> War of Independence database, 32:11/23-EOF

Oyārun looked up from the database and sighed. Of all the topics in the world, her mind had to fix itself upon Aramīn, well after she'd finished her homework and garnered an uncommon amount of praise from her teacher. This went beyond usual abuwen, special interests like floater races, public transport, or space weather. No, it had to be a person, a living person, a public figure, and Aramīn at that. Oyārun knew some people had specific persons as their abuwen and that this phenomenon was slightly more common among girls, but still she wished she could be somehow more ordinary. At least Aramīn did not displace her primary abuwen, paper folding. Yet.

Her fingers worked through the familiar motions, and one of her special creations took shape in her hands—the paper airplane that set the Eren-wide record of time aloft. It wasn't such a big deal: other than her, there were only seven people on the planetoid interested in paper airplanes, they didn't have a large enough hangar to practice airplane throwing, the air conditions could not be adjusted precisely enough ... and so on. Still, she was proud of the accomplishment. It wasn't a special accomplishment—it didn't improve on their living conditions or the volatile political situation, it didn't garner a lot of public interest, it didn't even help her find a career path. But at least it wasn't actively harmful.

She was beginning to suspect that her interest in Aramīn though would prove to be actively harmful. He was a Falconer, people said—another cognotype just as undesirable as Undesirables, the one that became the Ereni cognotype upon Independence. Her own cognotype. But Falconers were supposed to be dangerous in comparison, even if they weren't formally persecuted; maybe only because the Empire could not quite pin down the genetic basis to do so. Or maybe because there were fewer of them? She didn't know. She wasn't sure where the name had come from either—people commonly said that Falconers were more like falcons, merciless birds of prey. Cognotypes generally weren't named after animals, though she wasn't sure she could list some of the less common ones. She had never been interested in this topic. The Jaya cognotype was named after a researcher, but before that, hadn't it been named after some kind of small animal? She vaguely recalled people protesting about that, and she agreed with them. But no one was protesting about *Falconer*. She felt uneasy that she hadn't considered this before; she'd accepted everything at face value. Was this the goal of her civics assignments—questioning social assumptions?

She could not stop thinking of Aramīn. Was it this aspect of danger that he held in himself that allowed him to take that step? To force his will on a dithering, unformed high council? Certainly in the interest of equality and justice, but still . . . all that just to leave politics soon after?

Oyārun turned around in her seat and threw the plane at the wall. Hard. It crumpled and fell to the floor of her small room. She turned back, closed her eyes, and rubbed first her temples and then her scalp. She pulled her soft cotton cap back on, sighed, and submerged in the data supplied by her neural interface.

The more she read, the more certain she was that her abuwen was destructive and wrong. Most of the interviewees in the archives who talked about Aramīn were still alive, and she knew she could seek them out. Eren was a small place. They might even indulge her. But the interviews made her think it would be a bad idea to try to elicit information from these people. For the time being, she fiddled with the data at hand.

Interviews were the kind of soft qualitative data that were so hard to tackle, unlike air humidity or paper thickness. Still, she persevered. The interviews could be grouped into two categories, very sharply defined: people who said positive things about Aramīn and people who said negative things about him. There was very little in between.

She read the ones that seemed to be situated in this gray zone with especially strong interest. Amasewun, Inofu, Isanakewu . . .

She tried to bring up a social graph, but everyone was connected to everyone else—Ereni leadership had been a very tightly knit circle back then, just after the War of Independence. She wondered if there was a way to quantify social closeness with the data at her disposal.

She color-coded people: red for the ones who disliked Aramīn, blue for the ones who liked him, yellow for the ones who seemed to have mixed emotions about him. She hid the ones without interviews—mostly people who died shortly after independence. Some people had oral history as their abuwen, and they jumped on the politicians as soon as the initial chaos wore off. In some cases, literally jumped on them. Oyārun smiled briefly.

She stared at the jumble of primary colors. There had to be a way to organize the data! She returned to the interviews, eager for inspiration.

> *These days, people like to say that many of the nobility did support our efforts, quietly, from the background. I am skeptical. [P: 5v] During the months I was active in the resistance, I only met Armyn, and I hadn't even heard of any others. Armyn made a clean break with his house when he left the planet with us, so I'm not even sure he should count. [P: 3v] But he was there, always.*
>
> —Inofu ta Afurawī, Ereni Oral History Archives,
> War of Independence database, 45:26/1-4

Inofu spoke carefully and precisely, but the councilmember called Aramīn by his old, pre-independence name, Armyn, and that annoyed Oyārun. She chided herself: that had to have been because they'd known each other for a very long time. Unlike many others, Aramīn had never disavowed his pre-independence name and even picked an Ereni name that sounded similar. Calling him Armyn was a sign of familiarity.

She bit her lower lip as she sat up straight. That's it! She tried to list the interviewees who called him Armyn.

There were disappointingly few results. She suspected it wasn't as much because of a lack of familiarity—most of his coworkers survived the war, up north at the High Plains Research Institute—but more because most people were eager to get rid of every last bit of Emeki Imperial convention, from spelling to religious rituals. Still, she listed the ones who called him Armyn as close associates. She had to try a different tack . . .

His coworkers. Would they be the closest to him? Aramīn had no family, his family disowned him in his late teens—if they could've stripped him of his nobility and later his house leadership, they would've done so without hesitation. Oyārun had read the news articles from the period. Aramīn was disowned when he started to study medical science, a vocation entirely unbecoming to an Imperial noble. Blood and guts and tears . . .

She shivered, suddenly reminded of her own family. They never disowned her, but sometimes it felt to her that was because they hadn't even cared enough to do that. This was unfair, she reminded herself. Both her parents were running themselves ragged working in the civil engineering division. So much to plan, build, maintain . . . it wasn't fair to expect them to be in touch even after she'd moved out, old enough to have her own tiny living space.

She missed them, but she was frustrated. She had to get back to the data at hand. Even this qualitative analysis was easier than contemplating her own circumstances.

Did the institute have some sort of organizational diagram? She had to dig hard to come up with the structure during Aramīn's tenure, but eventually she managed. She could fill it with names, weight the links in the social graph with workplace closeness . . . would this work? She had no way of knowing who met each other regularly afterhours, who liked to chat in the lounge . . . she knew it was a long shot, but she had to try.

She listened to Aramīn's favorite music as she poked and prodded the data into shape.

> In the power to yield lies liberation
> We are here, resurfacing from the serpent seas
>
> —Ephemera: Serpent Seas

The answer was unexpected to Oyārun, though she reflected that it would probably have been obvious to anyone who knew Aramīn in person. The māwalēni who were trained by him, operated on by him, these people had positive reactions to him. His fellow researchers and other employees of HPRI were more likely to be averse to him the larger the organizational distance.

They said he tortured his charges. He was cruel. He was heartless.

His charges said he was cold, but fair, always very fair.

The rest was history: he left the planet, he left the Empire. He had nothing in common with his new chosen people. He wasn't a māwalēni himself, and he didn't have the Undesirable genotype either. He could've stayed on Emek since he wasn't marked for elimination or a lifetime of servitude, like most of those who fled. He joined the refugees because of . . . his conscience?

Did he have a conscience? Could he have a conscience? She tried hard to bridge the gap between unfamiliar cognotypes and social classes. He was an Imperial noble, even if of Plainsfolk origin. Had been a noble. He had worked extremely hard for the cause of independence. He helped build the country. But even the people who had positive attitudes toward him remarked that he was a sadist—"a Falconer even." She felt bad that a people whose cognotype used to be so reviled were now reviling another cognotype in turn. There had to be some kind of expression for this, but a few quick searches did not turn it up.

She couldn't wrap her head around any of this. She had to talk to some of these people to understand Aramīn. But was there a way to find an answer without talking, in general? She had to see for herself.

See.

She could see him. From a distance. See how he acted. Feel the impression his mind made on her, for she was a māwalēni herself. For a moment, she reflected on how she had the Undesirable genes at the same time. The former Undesirables were in the majority on Eren, and they were free from the Imperial yoke of Emek.

She was everything he wasn't. He was everything she wasn't. She had to see him for what he was.

She kept on listening to the music as she snuck out of her living quarters.

> *The stream never-ending,*
> *the overwhelming, the never-escape,*
> *white corridors*
> *the pain all-encompassing,*
> *everything is close;*
> *you are close . . .*
> *—Trees as Towers: The Never-Escape*

Oyārun turned the music down only as she approached the block where he lived: a neighborhood quite far but still looking much the same as her own, houses transformed from old miners' barracks and office buildings, crammed full of rooms barely large enough for a bed across. Aramīn was still an influential figure, but Eren was a very equal society. There wasn't much for anyone, and most resources went into maintaining life in a hostile environment. She'd heard enough from her parents to know that, from their arguments about "a lack of resources" in muffled tones well past her bedtime. There was never enough space.

She knew he was due back relatively soon. She sat down behind a chute and turned her attention inward. She read the latest paper-folding news, but her thoughts kept on drifting back to him. Besides, the latest talk about how to create large modular figures from oddly shaped packaging leftovers disillusioned her. Does freedom necessitate poverty, she wondered, and closed the news.

> *He was always spotlessly dressed. I used to work at HPR before the war, but when the hostilities broke out, I was stuck at the capital. And then I ran into him, just in, you know, this war zone. [P: 1.2v] In the middle of this war zone. [P: 0.7v] And he still looked, he was, you know, dressed unbelievably sharp. There was blood around and . . . [P: 0.5v] and dirt, and he was just there in the middle of it looking for all the world like, like he came from, I don't know, a court reception or something. No idea how he did it.*
>
> —Omoyedārō ta Beyun, Ereni Oral History Archives,
> War of Independence database 8E:2-8

Oyārun glanced up at the sound of steps approaching, refocused her attention. She pushed herself between the chute and a wall, hoping the shadows would hide her. He passed by her without noticing anything, but she was too scared to breathe a sigh of relief.

He was still spotlessly dressed, wearing an aubergine-colored overcoat over his rather generic dark-blue tunic and loose pants. She was surprised for a moment. Blue was the color of knowledge, information, the māwal, so it was understandable for him to be wearing it even if he was not a māwalēni himself. She wondered if that was what the dark shade signified. She never cared much about color symbolism. But aubergine . . . aubergine did not stand for anything. It was just a color, an uncommon one at that. The cut of the coat suited him exceptionally well, she thought and wondered if it was just her abuwen talking. Still, the coat looked custom-made, a rarity on the planetoid. How did he get ahold of it?

As the fear left her and her limbs slowly unfroze, she realized she had not paid any attention to his presence beyond the immediately prevalent visual details. She had to have perceived his mind because she didn't remember a lack, but she couldn't recall any details. Just the coat, one of its corners almost brushing her feet. His regal bearing. His firm, purposeful steps. Again, she hadn't even seen his face.

She called up his profile. His face was smooth and oval, his jawline small. He had single-lidded eyes and eyebrows that might have been touched up with liner or just uncommonly sharp. His skin was pale shading to brown, not pink— somewhat lighter than hers. His expression was elegant, even a trifle haughty. The large skullcap covering his bald head looked hand-embroidered, the same aubergine color decorated with a thick grayish-blue thread.

She wondered how long he'd taken until his profile picture looked just right. His appearance was probably very important to him if he could procure such an overcoat. The colors of his house had been teal and lilac, and aubergine was close. But he had no love to share with the court, and for him, his house had only been a tool to achieve his aims. Maybe, she thought, the coat was a way for him to assert his uniqueness?

Her thoughts ground to a halt. Footsteps from the opposite direction. He was coming back! Did he just drop something in his room and then head out again? His tasks were finished for the day. Where was he going?

Her fingers gripped each other so strongly that for a moment she was afraid her bones might snap. She desperately tried to imagine herself invisible. He passed by her again without noticing, went down the alley, and turned right.

She forced herself back on her feet. Her muscles protested. She had to go after him!

The first two steps were the hardest. Eventually, she fell into a rhythm of following him, like a game: halting when he did, ducking into side alleys and doorways, even predicting his moves. She wondered briefly if she was supposed to be bad at this because of her cognotype. It went smoothly, even though it felt improper.

He passed through an industrial area, and for a while, there was no cover that would hide her. She willed him not to look back. It seemed to work—as he was increasingly lost in thought. He strode along thin, snaking corridors, and she was shadowing him without difficulty. He wasn't paying any attention to his surroundings, she thought, but she kept herself as far from his mind as possible, due to some irrational fear that he might notice. He wouldn't have a correct sensation of being watched. He wasn't overly cautious either, at least as much as she could tell from the interviews. He himself had never been interviewed by the historians. Did he say no, or did no one ask him?

The corridor suddenly opened up to a large cavern—a hall, she corrected herself. He strode on. She halted just before the exit, peering outside. Memorial Park, she realized with a startle. But he had no family—?

Could she get any closer? She had to get closer! Fortunately, the carved memorial steles were chest-high and densely spaced. Many deaths in the war. She stepped among the steles and realized just what she had been thinking. *Fortunately?* She shuddered. Was Aramīn having a bad influence on her? She had to bring this to a close as fast as possible. Just as soon as she found answers to the questions burning inside her.

She weaved through the steles in a wide arc, ending just behind Aramīn. She peeked out from behind a stele and could see his back. He was standing in front of one of the many war memorials. A long list of names was etched into the stone.

He took a step backward—her body froze again—and bent forward from the waist. Again, a step backward, again a bow. A third time. She didn't recognize the ritual. Three steps forward, without bowing.

"In the name of the One Most High, exalted and elevated, transcendent and all-encompassing." His voice was sonorous but not particularly deep—just like in the rare recordings. She held on to the stele as she slowly, cautiously leaned out from behind it.

"You console the souls of the dead as you console the souls of the living. All the world is in the hollow of your palm, you, who inhabit the heights and the depths. I call out to you and beseech you, just as you called out to our ancestors to show them your paths."

It didn't sound like an Imperial ritual—the requests for the god-emperor's intercession were markedly missing. Was this a lesser house tradition? She called up her interface, tried to search for the phrases while he went on and on in a slow but steady pace with chant-like inflections. She found an exact match.

Mourning ritual for the head of the house, House Gubhas. Its origins are shrouded in mystery; its phraseology suggests that it was incorporated into Imperial lore from High Plains tradition. The performer of the ritual—in most cases, the new head of the house—directly addresses the One Most High, but despite this notable . . .

She skipped down.

The ritual is exceedingly lengthy—her heart sank—*as it is meant to allow the new head to reflect on the transitory nature of their position. The full mourning cycle lasts an Imperial year . . .*

She skimmed. How long would he stay here, reciting?

One performance of the ritual takes about an hour and a half. It is recited on alternate weekdays and certain Imperial holidays, most notably the . . .

She had time. She could wait. It was interesting anyway. She made herself running subtitles and quietly lowered herself on the ground, behind her stele.

He went on, never halting, never hurrying. While she couldn't see the text carved into the stele in front of him, the ritual frequently called for a mention of the name of the person. She just had to wait for it to come up.

"Ieyūni ta Enafisul, who died a violent death, who died at the hands of a murderer," the ritual had multiple versions for natural deaths, accidental deaths, assassination attempts . . . she reflected on how many ways there were for a head of a house to die. "Your blood calls out to us. Aye, we say your blood has not been shed in vain. You, the most noble of us . . ." She stopped paying attention as she frantically searched for the name. A secret lover? An illegitimate sibling? Or even a descendant? Court intrigue swirled in her head. And if the mourning cycle was only a year long, then why was he still saying these words? The war ended a long time ago.

Ieyūni ta Enafisul was apparently not a remarkable person, as Oyārun found very little data. She fought and died in the war. She had been a young māwalēni who managed to escape induction to the ranks of the Imperial Seers, then she went up to the High Plains and received some training at HPRI. She joined the Column-Tree Forest guerrilla bands and participated in several important strikes on the Southern Passageway and the neighboring towns south of the Forest. She died in an ambush alongside four of her comrades. There wasn't much else.

The lover theory looked the most likely—but wasn't Aramīn aromantic and asexual, like Oyārun herself? His profile clearly said so; this was one of the very few commonalities between the two of them. Oyārun bit down on her lower lip. She would have to ask around. Maybe someone remembered her. Maybe there was no more data because someone had been going around deleting information. Was that even possible?

She sat in silence, listening. After a while, her teeming thoughts quieted down, and she was drawn into the ritual. He recited with grace and precision. Whoever this mysterious Ieyūni was, her soul would clearly be satisfied. Even the One Most High would be satisfied.

She could feel herself slipping into a trance, but she didn't mind. The world narrowed down to Aramīn, to the sound of his voice. She thought she'd like him to pray for her too, and then she didn't think much at all.

The ritual came to a close, she noticed with an unexpected wave of sadness. Everything was transitory. Eventually, even mourning came to an end. He hadn't arrived from the direction where she was presently standing, so if she was lucky, he wouldn't notice her at all on his way out. Still, better get some distance between them. She got slowly back up on her feet—

Instead of turning around, he took a step back and bent forward from the waist, beginning anew. She was so surprised that her legs tangled together, seemingly of their own accord, and she toppled forward and hit the ground.

He turned around. Looked at her lying in a heap. She glanced up at him. He raised an eyebrow.

"Have you been spying on me?"

"I—no—I mean yes, but not like that—" She could feel her face redden as she babbled.

He chuckled softly. "Security does not seem to be running at peak capability today," he said, clearly amused.

She got on her knees. "I'm not a danger to you."

"Hmm?"

She got back up on her feet, brushed off her clothes with shaking hands. Looked at him. "I'm not a danger to you"—her voice trembled just as strongly—"so the fact that they didn't catch me means they were performing *well*, not the opposite." Why was she saying this? Why was she saying anything? She wanted to run away, but she felt rooted to the spot, and her mouth wouldn't stop blabbering.

He looked surprised for once and then . . . pleased? "Technically, yes"—he said and adjusted his overcoat with a minimal, automatic gesture—"but that's of course only true if you are indeed not a danger to me."

She had no idea what to say next. She had not even known he had a security detail! There was so much she didn't know about him. Her mind seemed to seesaw between trying to say everything at once and being so terrified she couldn't get a single word out. Her mouth opened and then closed.

He nodded slightly. "I suppose you're not a danger to my person." He paused. "Did you mean to talk to me?"

She nodded, speechless.

"Come closer. I don't bite." He held up both hands. "I won't touch you without your permission, I promise." He glanced around. "There is a bench toward the back. We can sit. Or we can go for a walk."

She held her ground.

"You know I'm not lying to you," Aramīn said. "You're a māwalēni, so you can sense it."

She blinked. "How did you know?"

"I can recognize the signs. I've seen many like you."

"And then you tortured them?" She felt like her entire body was on fire.

"I would not do anything to anyone without their consent," he said. He was telling the truth. The way he saw the truth, at least. After all, he didn't *force* the High Council to do anything either; he just shamed them into following him, she realized. But she did not share that shame, that Imperial guilt. Before independence, she would have been labeled both a Seer and an Undesirable. She stepped closer.

"A walk?" He turned around and strode ahead. She tagged along, still silent.

"What's your name?" He could've checked her profile for the answer. He was trying to make small talk, she realized with a sinking feeling.

"Oyārun," she said.

"What are you studying?"

"Pre-engineering subjects." She swallowed. She was so afraid of him, and he looked nonchalant. Patient with her. "A lot of math and physics mostly. I'm almost done with general studies." She tried not to think of her civics homework.

The paths among the steles were narrow, and she was glad she could only see his back. It made talking a lot easier.

"Which branches of engineering are you interested in?"

"I don't really . . . know yet." Another swallow. "I like aircraft. But they don't really . . . don't really . . ."

"See much use on Eren, you mean?" More of a statement than a question. With no hint of mockery in his voice.

"Yes, yes. So I don't really know. I thought I'd . . . look around. See what there is to do. Maybe something related to space travel." She sighed. "I've been putting it off." Why was she telling him this?

"I could invite you to my workplace," he said. "Plenty of work for engineers. Especially bioengineering, neuroengineering, but a little of everything. It might be something to aim toward. You will need to find an internship placement soon, and you might like this."

"S-sure. Thank you."

They walked ahead in silence. The hall was larger than she'd remembered. Eventually he offered, "That's not why you've sought me out."

"I . . . I just wanted to know." He didn't respond. "About you. What kind of person you were. I read . . . a lot." She took a deep breath. "I couldn't make sense of it."

He turned left. "That's the bench I was talking about. If you would like to sit."

They sat with more than enough room between them. She stared straight ahead at a small empty space in the maze and the small fountain in the center of it. There were more steles in the hall than she'd thought and only a few scraggly trees.

"This is the only fountain on Eren," he said, not looking at her.

"You know this place very well." She felt foolish for saying such a triviality.

"I come here every day."

"Who was Ieyūni?"

"One of my charges."

She blinked, stunned. When she'd stumbled, he was about to start the whole ritual over again with a different name. "Do you say prayers for every one of them?"

"I try to." He leaned back. "I aim to finish in this lifetime." For a moment, sorrow and regret tinted his voice. Just for a moment.

Her thoughts raced. He had to have trained hundreds of people. He surely didn't only mean everyone he had commanded because he had never commanded a unit where Ieyūni was serving.

"You're very . . . different from what I'd expected," she said.

He raised an eyebrow again—she could tell without looking. He waited for her to speak.

"People said you were a Falconer," she said after some hesitation. She didn't know of a less harsh term, the way *Ereni cognotype* had supplanted *Undesirable*.

"Oh, I suppose I do have those tendencies." He looked up at the domed ceiling high above. "It's a spectrum, you know. Just like the Ereni cognotype." So eerily calm, she thought. "I never even hunted for sport. I don't go around murdering people. We are all different."

It was out of her mouth before she knew it. "Would you like to?"

"To murder people?" His calm did not waver.

She was sure he'd take offense. Then she realized that everything she could say, everything hurtful, someone must have said to him already. She saw those people in the archives. She felt her face burn in embarrassment. He went on, and she was sure he was only pretending not to notice her reaction.

"I'm not interested. If I were to murder someone, it would be all over," he said.

"All over?"

He closed his eyes. She turned to look at him. "Control," he said after a while. "I need control."

"Over people?"

"Yes." He opened his eyes and turned his head slightly to look at her, a gracefully understated movement. He had known perfectly well that she'd look at him—he had known it so well that he didn't even need to think of it. He automatically adjusted his behavior to take advantage of his situation. To reach his aims.

"Complete control," he said, his gaze fixed on her.

She looked away, flustered. She tried to sound similarly nonchalant. "So . . . do you enjoy causing people pain?"

"Yes, I do." As if he was being quizzed by a teacher. An easy question. "I'm a sadist, after all. That's different from being a Falconer. People of any cognotype can be sadists." He paused a bit. "Even yours."

Was he goading her? She had to stay calm, calmer than this. Her mind held on to that template of question and answer, of education and teachers. She could get through this conversation without her heart jumping out of her chest if she thought of it as quizzing him. She went on.

"And you did cause them pain."

"I *do* cause them pain," he corrected her.

"Why are you answering my questions?"

"I have time, and I find them interesting." So detached. That was the word: he felt permanently detached. And yet probably more in tune with his surroundings than she herself ever would be, she suspected.

"So you . . . ask them to allow you. To cause them pain."

"Yes."

"And they allow you."

"Yes."

"Why?"

She could feel he was about to say, *What do you think?*—but he changed his mind at the last moment.

"I want them to be perfect." He leaned forward. "I can improve on them. The best they can offer—I can help them achieve it. I want my charges to be perfect. You see?" A glimmer of eagerness. She realized he didn't have very strong emotions, in general. She nodded.

"So we make a deal. They give themselves over to me. And I make them perfect. As much as I can." He did not take his eyes off her. "Everyone benefits."

It did make a twisted sort of sense to her. "But there is pain."

"No transformation is ever without pain," he said. A quote from somewhere? She blinked. "You've found your niche."

"I have." His gaze seemed questioning. "Are my answers bothering you?"

She returned his gaze. "Why are you so honest?"

"I have always been honest."

"I thought people like you often lied."

A trace of a smile. "I have no need to lie."

2.

Oyārun knew all too well that she should study—she had quite an amount of math to review for her next meeting with her teacher—but instead she just sat, alone and in silence, replaying her sensory logs of the conversation with Aramīn.

Her tiny living quarters were like a shirt, overly tight around her body.

Did she finally understand what kind of man he was? She only knew that her abuwen showed no signs of subsiding. The more she knew about him, the more she wanted to know. Then again, this was a common characteristic of abuwen even when they were not person-focused. Would the process ever run its course?

Aramīn had invited her to see his workplace, reiterating the offer when the two of them had said goodbye. She had to overcome her fear of unfamiliar situations and make that visit; her own mind would not give her rest until then.

She would love to work with him. As an engineer. As—

She swallowed hard.

Her fingers folded and unfolded a scrap of paper, over and over again.

Her mind stopped. Time stopped.

She had to make that visit.

She took a deep breath, shut down playback, called up her organizer. On top, the random quote of the day from her favorite poems said, "Rip open the seal release the magic."

She blinked. She was sure the random quote had been something completely different just a moment ago. Had she overlooked it? She checked her system logs. Nothing seemed out of the ordinary.

She closed the organizer, got up—the chair toppling over—and rushed out, the echoes of the poem reverberating in her head.

> Rip open the seal release the magic;
> everything I can offer to draw you close
> is in the tiniest inflections of my voice—
> I am myself, and you—you abide in me
> until even the sunsets turn into dust . . .
>
> —The Blessings of the Path by Omasārun ta Idarawul,
> third stanza

It was early in the morning; Oyārun was stunned to realize how early. Sleep and wakefulness had blended together. How much time had passed since her meeting with Aramīn? Three days—it was hard to fathom. Three days spent in a daze. If anyone had tried to contact her, she hadn't noticed. She had to bring this to a close, force it if need be.

She struggled to keep herself from breaking into a run. Her muscles were taut and rigid. The Institute was close by. After all that time, it was still called the Institute, a reminder of the High Plains of Emek forever and ever. A place of sanctity, a place of pain and blood and sacrifice. The High Plains far away, on another planet, in another solar system. The Institute remained, carrying the name ever onward into the future.

She walked right in, no one stopping her. She hesitated to check—the place was still restricted-entry—but someone had put her onto the visitor list. Did Aramīn seriously think she would come to see him? Did he truly want that? Did he expect her?

She ran along white corridors, without realizing where she was going. She only stopped when she painfully bumped into someone—

The young māwalēni stared at her in surprise. Oyārun opened her mouth to apologize, but the māwalēni held up a hand, silenced her.

"Are you looking for some—oh. Aramīn? I can show you the way to his office."

Oyārun nodded and belatedly closed her mouth.

"I am Emien," the māwalēni said. She was young—and exhausted-looking, maybe just a year or two older than her. Dark semicircles stood out on the pale skin underneath her eyes. "Sorry, apparently someone forgot to clear you for the floor plans." She closed her eyes for a second; when she reopened them, a craving for sleep hit Oyārun. "All done."

Oyārun murmured thanks and called up a copy of the floor plans.

"I can show you the way," Emien said. "I'm going in that direction anyway."

Oyārun nodded gratefully.

The two of them walked without saying much, Oyārun behind Emien. The māwalēni was wearing a long-sleeved white smock, matching trousers, and a white bandana. The smock had a turtleneck collar—Oyārun strained her eyes, trying to see the implants peeking out from underneath the fabric. She stopped when she realized Emien had noticed; Oyārun didn't mean to be rude, she was simply curious. Anything to take her mind off the constant, immense fear.

Emien halted, and Oyārun almost fell over her. "His office is at the end of this corridor," Emien said and pointed right. "I'm going left here."

Oyārun wanted to say something, but the words wouldn't come out. Emien was about to walk away but noticed her distress and stopped. She looked at Oyārun, head tilted to one side. "Mhm?"

"I—what do you think of him?"

"Huh? Oh, he's all right. A bit on the strict side, but all right." Emien looked concerned all of a sudden. "You heard those stories? That was just Imperial propaganda." She rolled her eyes. "Trash for the yellow rags. Trust me, he's all right." She spoke with conviction and made no attempt to hide or camouflage her feelings.

Oyārun gulped. They said goodbye and Oyārun walked down the corridor. Twenty-one steps altogether; twenty-one steps of mind-numbing fear.

Oyārun pushed the door open. It yielded, and she realized she had forgotten to knock. Embarrassment froze her, and she stood still, unthinking. The walls were thick, and the doorway surrounded her. She felt boxed in.

"Do come in," Aramīn called out to her.

When she didn't move, he got up from his seat and walked toward her. "I thought we'd already established that I'm not one for eating people," he said cautiously.

She walked in, her legs stiff like wooden sticks.

"Do sit."

She was frozen.

"Here, I have a chair for you," Aramīn said and stepped to the wall, picked up one of the chairs, and put it behind her. "You can sit now." His voice was smooth and reassuring. She sat.

He sat on top of his desk; it was mostly empty. He threaded his fingers together. "So you've come to see the Institute for yourself. I'm happy to show you around. A little good-natured propaganda is not beneath me," he said with a small, sarcastic smile.

She nodded, one of the vertebrae in her neck cracking. She could see he was trying to put her at ease.

"I was just reviewing a new procedure proposed by one of our surgery teams. It's probably not really up your alley. We can go and look around. I can show you the—"

She broke in. "No, no, it's all right—" She didn't want to keep him from anything, especially not his work. Besides, everything he said was interesting.

"Oh?" He raised an eyebrow. "Would you be interested?" He smiled again, a hungrier smile. Just for a moment. "Ah, is it that everything about me is equally fascinating to you?"

She had a hard time believing he was not a māwalēni himself. Were her reactions to him so transparent? They probably were, she decided. Or maybe he had just a little grasp of the māwal but used that to all its worth.

When no answer was forthcoming, he said, "Well then. I cannot promise this will hold your attention, but I'll do my best to explain everything." He leaned back and shared his mental workspace with her with a command.

It was just a casual gesture for him, but for Oyārun it carried an intimacy beyond what would usually be attributed to it. Maybe because, for her, there was no clear-cut division between input from her computer interface, input from her senses, and input via the māwal—it all blended together, and thus even when he simply shared something with her via purely technological means, it was as if he'd opened his mind to her without hesitation.

She was touched, despite thinking it unreasonable. He didn't seem to notice. She leaned forward as he began his explanation.

"I should offer some context first. My apologies if we tread familiar terrain, in the beginning at least."

She nodded again to show it was all right. She appreciated his consideration.

"All right. Eren is an extremely high-māwal zone, and we need to spend a lot of effort on maintaining a habitable environment," he said. It sounded like a quote from a lecture. He probably lectured often, she thought. "We need a large contingent of māwalēni whose primary task is to make sure no serious problems occur. This is why the Empire originally abandoned Eren, even though it was set to be a lucrative mining colony. It's necessary—"

He got up and began to circle her chair, talking all the while. The effect was mesmerizing.

"It's necessary to loosely bind together and harmonize the minds of everyone in general society and exert a stabilizing influence. In an environment that can be shaped by people's expectations and fears, a single person's panic can cause runaway reactions if precautions are not taken."

He stopped directly behind her, the tone of his voice abruptly changing.

"Did you know the first people to live here were devoured by monsters?"

She offered a weak no.

"It's not hidden from those who choose to investigate, but it's generally held that it's for the best if people do not investigate." He sighed and began his circle anew. "These days we can prevent such large-scale disasters without inhibiting māwal use. But it takes a lot of effort, and all too many of our māwalēni are busy with this constant struggle. We're trying very, *very* hard to make sure that people who choose to join us can perform to the best of their ability, and possibly beyond. We are very short-staffed. It's the only way. This is the System of Eren, not as you'd hear of it but as it is. And if people had not already worked their hardest, I would not have had my moment of fame."

Oyārun thought back on the video. All the weapons in the crowd. The emotions running high. And yet, the quiet, the people turning to each other to help. She nodded.

He looked at her, and his gaze went to her marrow. "We only take volunteers. We are very firm about this. Believe me." He looked away. "Still. I'm not proud of some of the things we do. We take people and squeeze them dry." His gaze flickered around the room, as if searching for a window to stare out. There was no window, and outside—she knew—no nature to behold, only a desert of rocks and silt. No air above the thick roofs of the domes.

He spoke with his back to her. "They die far too young. And they die all spent. Back on Emek, when the Imperial Seers were all spent satisfying the whims of the noble houses, my blood had boiled with righteous anger."

She couldn't imagine him boiling with anything, but she could feel there was indeed an undercurrent of emotion beneath the surface: not particularly strong, but steady and never ceasing. He went on.

"Now we do the same ourselves. Do you understand that?"

Silence.

"There's no place for us to go," she said after she could overcome her hesitation. "This is our planet now . . . this is the price of independence." She wished she could believe that herself.

"But this is too high a price. I do not want to see them die. I made an oath I would dedicate all my efforts to this. I cannot—" He didn't finish the sentence.

A flash of insight struck Oyārun: Aramīn could not stand to feel useless. He wanted to be in control. Was all this about him and his mastery of his surroundings, by proxy? Even if it was, his efforts were still for a worthy cause, Oyārun decided.

"Let's get back to the diagrams," Aramīn said and turned around. His face was inscrutable. "These are quite drastic procedures."

Did he have trouble speaking?

"To amplify the māwal?" she offered.

"No, no," he shook his head. "On this planet, we have all the amplification we need, and then some more. And with the people we recruit, lack of power is simply not an issue. This is all for regulation."

She didn't really get the idea. They hadn't gotten to anything similar yet in her classes.

"Many māwalēni can raise a large amount of māwal, here on Eren. Training or no training, implants or no implants. But that's just a burst, or some kind of runaway reaction, a positive feedback loop that runs until some limiting factor is hit. What we need is constant, steady high throughput."

She had heard of positive feedback loops but not too much—she knew "positive" didn't mean the loop was desirable, only that it was amplificatory. Still, she got the gist of what he was saying. She nodded, her neck no longer clicking and creaking.

"This necessitates constant control and considerable effort. Especially since ideally there should be a division between power raising and power direction."

"Um?"

"Power raising and power direction, at their most focused, are hard if not impossible to do concurrently for a single mind. It is much more fruitful to split the functions, assign them to separate people."

He breathed out. She breathed out too and blinked. Had their breaths unconsciously synchronized? Was that a good sign, or the exact opposite?

"This helped us to persist here," he said, suddenly aloof. He held up one hand, looked at it. Showed it to her. "You know, my hands are bloody."

She sat in silence. She knew that—everyone knew—everyone knew everything. Back then, politics; now, history. She didn't know how to react. Independence had been hard-won.

He looked upward, toward a nonexistent sky. "And yet you still come to me." Then he shook his head and cleared his throat. He didn't speak for a long time.

Her mind spun. Was this a prescheduled confession? Or was it more spontaneous? She could not tell. His sadness, however, was genuine. Not strong, and mixed with a kind of self-reflective amusement—"Am I really feeling this?"—but genuine nonetheless.

"Enough," he said. "We have a task at hand."

3.

Oyārun sat, looking at the little fountain—the only one of its kind. She felt empty, and at the same time, weighed down, as if something were steadily pressing on her shoulders, pushing her chest cavity inward . . .

Aramīn had shown her the schematics, explained everything in detail. But when it was time for her tour of the building, he demonstrated a curious reluctance.

She was turning her mental impressions around in her head; it was all surprisingly difficult. Eventually, she concluded Aramīn had assumed she would be discomforted. That she would disapprove. But why would that bother him?

A thought—

She was an outsider. She was not one of his charges and was not slated to become one.

Maybe he was afraid of—

She could not pursue this train of thought any further.

She clutched her arms around her chest, hugged herself tightly. She didn't . . . she didn't want to think of it. She knew, knew for once that *he* would not want her to think of it. She squeezed her eyes shut.

Then she blinked. How had she gained so much insight into one person? Certainly, via the māwal . . . but the Ereni cognotype did not lend itself to such approaches. She could perceive the māwal, and that probably helped, but still . . .

"It's the sheer effort I put into it," she said out loud. "Into understanding him." No one was there to hear her. Her voice sounded too low and deep for her ears. "It's the sheer effort," she repeated.

This took her mind away from the rest.

Oyārun tried to wrangle Aramīn into an internship placement. She was surprised by her own audacity. It was all just text messages sent back and forth, and not very long ones at that, but this was not something she would've imagined herself capable of doing.

It's the fear, she thought without pausing to examine the source of her fear.

Life sped up, and she moved through it in a daze, staggering from one day to another. Her conversations with the people she'd met through paper folding lessened and then ceased. Her meetings with her teacher were shorter and shorter. She wasn't sure when she'd last talked to her parents.

She would start her internship at the end of the short cycle. Just a few more days.

She felt a craving, yet she did not know what it was she craved.

They were not, strictly speaking, visions; they only had a tactile component. Oyārun felt herself strapped to some kind of—machine? frame?—and she felt the straps tighten. A warm, dry hand smoothed over her brow. Then she was lying in a soft and firm bed, and all around there was white. That emptiness was the only thing she saw.

She wondered if she should seek help, ask for a counseling appointment—

but what would she say? That something was swimming below the surface, waiting to break out, and she had glimpsed the shadow of its body, rising from the depths to lurk just below the edges of her consciousness, a sea monster determined to ascend? How would she say that? And was that even a problem in itself, or was it something she simply needed to come to terms with, something perfectly natural and right, if somewhat unusual?

The māwal would give her visions. Surely this was expected, especially on this planet, and especially given that she was sensitive to it.

Then why the sense of urgency?

Her time frame shortened. She counted every hour until the day she would set foot in the Institute again. She kept on feeling, and then rejecting the feeling, that her life would be over.

This was to be a simple junior internship in medical engineering, nothing more.

She tried to tell herself that.

That was before she came face-to-face with Aramīn and found herself making that unspeakable request.

4.

Aramīn went pale, all the blood draining from his cheeks. Yet he kept his composure. "Sorry, would you please say that again?" he said with such forced evenness in his voice that a chill ran along Oyārun's spine.

"I want to join the System," she said.

There. She had done it. Even that morning when she woke, she had told herself she wouldn't. It was impossible that she would even entertain such a thought.

But she wanted to, she craved it so much it was impossible to describe—

"You only say that because you are obsessed with me," he said with cruelty sharp as a knife. He wanted to push her away.

"No, I—" How was she supposed to respond to that? To such a slur? Yes, she was indeed *obsessed*, if that was the word he wanted to use—instead of something like *special interest* that was more neutral, or *abuwen*, actually positive. "I am, I am, I admit that, but that has nothing to do with this—"

"No?" He leaned forward. Eyes narrowing. "The way I see it, you grew up, acquired enough of a grasp on the māwal to be able to function, and you never felt attracted to it. You knew what it was, but it was not your path." Longer and longer pauses between words. *Not. Your. Path.* "And then all of a sudden," his words hissed, "you become obsessed with me, and you realize this is what you need to keep me close. Suddenly, you want to join the System."

He stood, right in front of her. He was taller than her, and she had to arc her neck uncomfortably upward.

"Let me tell you something," he said. "We fought so that you would not have to do this. We fought so that no one would be forced to do this. We fought for your right of choice. Many of us died for your right of choice. We fought, *and we won*. I will not . . . I will *not* allow you to throw that away."

She took a step back, and her feet tangled in the chair behind her, sitting there unused. She lost her balance and fell—

He grabbed her arms and steadied her. Then he dropped his arms and looked away.

"I'm sorry. I shouldn't have acted in a threatening way. But I can only say this much, and I can only say it thus. For you, this is history, but for me, it was my entire life."

"I'm sorry—" she began but stopped, not knowing how to continue.

"We fought so that the Imperial Seers would not have to live their lives in servitude to the Court. We fought so that the Undesirables would not be eradicated. You are both, yet you would throw this freedom away." End of the sentence. End of the line. He paused. "I will not allow it."

She braced herself. Then she stepped around him, in his line of sight, and stared him in the face. "This is what I want to do." She saw something there, and she added, on impulse", "This is what you want to do."

He looked as if slapped.

She went on, just as merciless as he had been.

"This is what you want to do." She imagined her eyes piercing his. She put force behind her gaze, willed it to be so. "You are flattered." She started to walk around him in a tight semicircle just like he had done but a little too close for comfort. She kept up eye contact all the while in a mechanistic but still all too effective manner. "I know how you see me. I'm young. I'm ideally suited to this. You are permanently, desperately short-staffed. I'm here to give you just what you want, and if my reasons are less than pure, *so are yours*. You might want to save the settlement, but that's not what *drives* you. What drives you is my obedience, the obedience of people like me, and now you are torn—turn me away and enjoy my obedience for a moment or keep me close and enjoy it for as long as I live."

He looked—taken aback?

"That . . ." He cleared his throat. "That might not be long."

She would not take her gaze off him, she would not let up for an instant—and he, he could not look away.

"I am here for you to do as you please. I know the risks. I know what's involved." She took a deep breath. "Let me help."

"You don't know," he said, looking away for a moment. Reminiscing? "You think you do, but you don't. You might understand the process, but you've never experienced the pain."

Despite his words, she could feel that inside him, something had given way, yet she was too caught up in her own fervor to rejoice.

He looked at her again. He had apparently used that moment to regain his composure, for he was just as forceful as before and probably twice as forceful as she had just been.

"I can take you. You are right. I am flattered, and you are well-suited to this line of work. But that's not why I'm taking you." His eyes bore into hers. Was he miming *her*? "I'm taking you because we, the collective *we*, do not have the *luxury* of turning any suitable person away. I have slapped you in the face and you have slapped me in the face. We are even."

His tone was abrasive, but she felt it was only an act. Inside, deep down inside, he was relieved. He was looking forward to this. He was—may the One Most High help them both—hungry.

II.

1.

"We'll also need an endorsement from your closest relatives," the brown-skinned young man with Worowan features said and scratched his hairless scalp under his cap. Oyārun was surprised to see the gesture in someone so young-looking. He must've been born off-Eren, must've had ample time to get used to the feeling of hair covering his head to feel the lack so acutely.

Oyārun transferred the documents. Her father had approved everything. On the call, he had looked even more tired than Emien. She felt the planetoid was eating everyone alive.

The man nodded to himself as he examined the documents. She looked at his profile—his name was Isinaiyu, and he had indeed been born elsewhere. He was also older than she'd guessed.

"Everything looks all right," he finally said. "I assume you haven't changed your mind . . .?"

She sighed. "It has been two weeks. I haven't changed my mind in two weeks, and I'm not going to change it now."

He shrugged, and she felt that he'd seen *that* already, people changing their minds at the very last instant . . .? It was a complicated feeling and she had trouble parsing it.

"All right, I'm clearing you for the medical," he said. "Go on ahead. Third floor, the corridor on the left." He made a little gesture with his fingers, and a path traced itself on her interface overlay. Such a deeply ingrained gesture, she thought. None of the stiffness of those born off-Eren, the older generation. How odd. But some people were more flexible than others.

She followed the path.

The doctor running the checks also looked Worowan: a short, stout woman with a spring in her steps. Her skin was much darker than Oyārun's. She introduced herself as Esesewi, and they greeted each other in the Worowan manner, grabbing the forearms and bowing their heads. Oyārun's family were mostly Plainsfolk, but she knew the basic Worowan customs from their neighbors in their housing unit.

Oyārun could feel the doctor making a preliminary assessment based on that single greeting: the texture and temperature of her skin, the steadiness—or, rather, unsteadiness—of her movements, the strength of her grip. All with effortless expertise.

"The examination is not particularly invasive," Esesewi said. Her voice was warm and deep, a welcome feeling among the cold walls. "Your interface gathers most of the relevant information already, so I just need a data dump. Give me root?"

She did. Esesewi went on talking while she examined the data. She described the additional tests: just a few simple cognitive tasks, and the detailed workup would be done concurrently with the new set of modifications once Oyārun passed the medical. Then the doctor looked directly at her, away from the readouts supplied by her interface. "By the way, you know I'm supposed to dissuade you?"

Oyārun shrugged. "You're the second person today."

Esesewi chuckled. "No point in it then?" She grinned at her. "I haven't said I wanted to dissuade you or that I would attempt to dissuade you, only that I was supposed to dissuade you. As far as I'm concerned, if you want to do this, that's just fine." She focused on the data again. "You will want out, but that will happen after the point of no return, you know?"

A wave of sudden fear ran through her. "I'm—"

"Look, it happens to almost everyone. I've been here a long time. It happens over and over. Now you'll just have to decide whether to go with your true will as opposed to your will at a given moment."

She wasn't sure she understood that. "Decide?"

"That happens right before the point of no return. You decide your true will and hand us the ability to enforce it. Even against yourself." The doctor sighed. "We wouldn't do this if the process was reversible or if it could be stopped, paused. But once started, it needs to run its course. It's dangerous to interrupt— dangerous for you, for us, for everyone. You can say no before, you can say no afterward, you can quit at any time, but you can't say no during the process itself." She spread her hands. "I'm sorry."

Oyārun hugged herself. A cold sensation was forming inside her, pulling her innards together like a black hole. "I'm—" She looked down. The floor was smooth and gray. "I mean that makes sense. I'm just afraid."

Esesewi glanced up. "We expect people to be afraid. I'd be worried for you if you weren't."

Aramīn looked down on his bare desk, his expression contemplative. He was mulling over the data, Oyārun knew. The medical, the more recent tests, her former data back from when she'd decided she would not train as a professional māwalēni—such a long time ago, shortly after her power had begun manifesting in earnest. They had taught her how to channel it away in safe ways, how to ask for help. They had set up a few simple mechanisms in her mind so that she wouldn't be troubled by the power she'd been born with, but that had never particularly interested her. She had had free choice every step of the way, and she had said no. But then, she changed her mind . . .

"This was a very clean job," Aramīn said, looking up at her. "You had no trouble in everyday life, is that correct?"

"It was fine." She felt embarrassed for a moment. "Sometimes I'd have these odd feelings, not even premonitions . . . forebodings maybe? But it was fine. Also, I had enough to help me make sense of what people were thinking but not so much to cause problems, so . . . the helpful parts without the troublesome parts?"

Aramīn nodded gravely. "Most people come to us when the bindings wouldn't hold or the power becomes unmanageable for some other reason." He stood and began to pace again. "I have to say I'm troubled by that. It mars the quality of consent. It's also a failing on our behalf."

"I didn't come because of that," Oyārun said. "I was fine."

"I know. Your motivations trouble me for other reasons." He was with his back to her, but she could feel his consternation, drawing from a source deep enough that she couldn't sense it without prying. She wouldn't pry.

He went on. "You're here because of your interest in me. It appeals to me, I must say. And I can certainly train you as I've trained many others. But I don't think I can truly give you what you desire." He stopped right behind her. "I don't have abuwen. I have a different cognotype, so I don't know this from personal experience. But I know that despite their intensity, sometimes they pass all of a sudden. The impact of the decision you are making now will last much longer."

Oyārun looked up at him, craning her neck. "Are there people who . . ." She wasn't even sure how to phrase it. "Who want to do it for its own sake?"

Aramīn stepped away from the chair, and she couldn't follow him with her gaze. "Oh, yes," he said. "Some even have it as their abuwen. But let's get back to you." He circled her and sat back up on the top of his desk. "You are good at power raising. Not much at control, of course, since you haven't trained at all. So we'll emphasize power raising if that's agreeable with you."

She nodded eagerly. Aramīn looked at her askance. "I suspect that at this point everything I say is going to be agreeable with you." He shook his head. "What shall I do with you?"

She was dressed in a plain white shirt and pants. She'd expected she'd have to wear something more ornate for the initiation. Many, many people had formal dress as their abuwen, and it showed. Every single function or event on Eren had its complicated rules of dress, every little fold and embroidery carried reams of meaning.

White symbolized emptiness.

She took a deep breath and opened the door to the small waiting room.

Aramīn was waiting for her, standing up from one of the many cheap, mass-produced chairs littering the HPRI building. Aramīn followed her gaze to the chair. "We make do with what we have," he said gravely. "Come."

She stepped closer and saw he was holding a roll of some kind of tape or ribbon in his hand.

"This is to symbolize your submission to my will and my control," he said. "For the duration of our cooperation. That is, if you are still willing."

"It's why I'm here." Her words felt too overwrought, too verbose. She took a breath. "Yes," she said.

Aramīn didn't miss the subtlety. He nodded appreciatively and smiled, a brief interruption in the ashen solemnity of his emotions.

"Turn around."

She did so.

"Your hands, please." After a moment of confusion, she put her hands behind her back, and he tied them together, the fabric of the red ribbon adhering seamlessly to itself. It didn't stick to her skin. She experimentally pulled her hands apart, but the ribbon held.

"This might be intense," Aramīn said, but he didn't pause. He put another strip of red ribbon around her neck. Her breath caught, and she didn't understand why—the ribbon wasn't tight, it fit just the right way—

It seemed right. It seemed proper.

She could feel Aramīn's hands, hesitating midair for a moment. Then he cleared his throat and led another red strip down her back along her spine, tying the loops around her neck and hands together. Finally, he made a handle for himself at the end of a long strip, affixed between her hands, and he led her out into the hall.

The white hall was smaller than she'd expected. She recognized some people: Esesewi, standing to one side, the bright white lights overhead creating highlights on her now-serious face, Emien, gangly and sleep deprived. People she'd come across in HPRI, casual acquaintances, always glad to see her even if weary and exhausted.

Aramīn walked up to a small dais with Oyārun and stood in front of her.

Two large, muscular people stepped to her sides, and one person walked up behind her. She was surrounded.

"Why have you come here?" Aramīn asked, so softly and gently that she yanked her head up and stared at him in amazement.

Then she realized she didn't know the words of the ritual. She shuddered. She opened her mouth, but she didn't know what to say.

"Just answer with your own words," Aramīn added and nodded encouragingly.

She swallowed. Her throat felt completely dry. "I've come here to join the System," she said as simply as she could. Fewer possibilities for error that way. She struggled to think clearly despite the all-consuming fear.

"Is it your true will to join the System?" he declaimed.

She nodded and said yes.

"Do you give me the ability to enforce your true will upon yourself when it is perilous to stop?"

She was about to answer, but he held up a hand. "Wait. After you've said yes, there won't be any turning back. I want you to know that." He looked at her like—like a daughter? No, something else, some other relation. Her head swam. "Do you understand?"

She nodded silently.

He raised his voice again. "What is your answer?"

"My answer is yes."

Aramīn nodded to the assistants. They stepped to her and gripped her arms, her shoulders. They held her in place.

"The people of the Free State of Eren support you," he went on. "The people are here to catch you if you stumble and fall. You will not have to face the pain alone." He paused.

She shuddered. The assistants held her strong.

"With the power vested in me by the people of Eren and the Ways," he stepped forward and placed a hand on top of her bare head, "I take control."

His voice had—if not his own māwal—the power of the ages and the expanses behind it. Her legs gave way. The people didn't allow her to fall to her knees. Her shoulders hurt as she was held up.

Aramīn went on. "I swear I will only act for the benefit of all sentience. I swear I will only cause pain when necessary, and I will not subject you to anything beyond your capacity to handle, as far as I can estimate."

He took his hand off her head and pulled out a small implement from the folds of his clothing. A—dagger of some sort? With some kind of force field in place of the blade. Her eyes flickered to the blade, to his face, to his fingers gripping the handle all too strongly—

"This is to remind me of my oath," he said and rammed the blade into his open palm.

Her breath caught. The field did not wound, there was no blood, no scar—but a whip of pain ran through his entire body, so intense that Oyārun could not help feeling it herself.

"I know what I demand," he said in an undertone. "Remember, always remember, I will only cause pain when necessary."

He yanked her chin up and pushed the blade into the middle of her forehead.

She screamed, her screams resonating inside her skull, and she fell, fell into darkness, and the people held her strong and would not let go.

2.

Oyārun was floating, her body out of sync with her mind. Was she lying on a bed? Was she—

Aramīn's words circled in her head, and she knew she had to hold on to them, preserve their meaning at all costs. The scene played in her head, over and over, in a loop. She no longer understood the words.

Spiders, insects, mythical aliens of yore, he had said. *Symbolic of the phylogenetically oldest parts of the nervous system, the ones most inaccessible to acting consciousness. Aversion is normal. In general, one does not want the acting consciousness to trespass there.*

Most of the time, that is. A flicker of a smile. *You will need to go there. You will need to welcome these parts into yourself. Give yourself over. We will keep you safe.*

We will keep you safe.

She made an attempt to reach out. Her arms were tied down with wide straps, and the feeling of the out-of-phase representation of her hand reaching out and passing through the straps spooked her. Where was she? What was going on? She knew she was supposed to remember. Was this an out-of-body experience? Could she simply float away?

She found it harder and harder to keep a hold on her consciousness—until it simply drifted away, her drifting away with it, floating on the streams, bobbing up and down.

It was black and gleaming like chitinous shapes; it was white and porous, desiccated; it was metallic quicksilver, protean, ever changing. It was translucent.

It reached out to Oyārun with sharp thin legs, and as she moved closer, she saw the legs ended in talons, but she knew it was good this way. She did not feel the supposed aversion.

Ten-eight, looking nominal so far.

Still, keep an eye on sublayer E for adverse reactions.

She only knew, with a certainty of ages-old declarations, the bedrock of civilization, that while it was fundamentally alien and inhuman, it was a part of her, now and forever, extending into all dimensions of time and space.

If it was her, then the only natural impulse was to unify, merge, draw it close.

It wanted to eat her, and she knew she had to be cut apart and consumed. That was why she was there in this fogged-over landscape extending into infinity—

It needed to devour her, and she could feel its urgency, in her stomach, in her chest. In the core.

It needed to flay her first.

So many sharp legs!

Spiking over F2. Looks nice and clean.

Yes, excellent response . . . very clean so far.

Cutting and slicing, holding fast.

Blood flowing ever so slowly as if time itself gradually came to a halt.

The pain was there, but the pain was good. It was only a part of the process, and it showed the process itself had not ceased to move along—

it wanted to merge, to pull apart the muscles and nestle close—

bursting out into millions of tiny tendrils, lodging itself in the flesh—

pulling apart the spinal column, running up golden-yellow and burning hot into the brain, all of a sudden very fast—

searing mere thought with its touch, and she screamed, screamed, and screamed—

Of course, proceeding as planned.

There was only her and the being, alien and immense, an impenetrable monolithic sentience come face-to-face with her. There was nothing else.

It was so much bigger than her!

Yet she could not shirk away. It was inside her, it was her, it was beautiful and hungry.

She gave in.

Oyārun was lost in the moment. How much time had passed? She was still there, face-to-face, merging, howling in pain and in raw, bare need, holding it close and being cut apart. People were speaking, passing messages. So many levels of the real, and she could pass between each of them with the barest thought, the faintest gesture . . .

She was tied to a machine, some kind of complicated apparatus with many thin-limbed surgical instruments issuing forth from a central hub—

the spider was eating her, feasting on her, embedding itself in her—

She's taking well to the implantation. Switching to DF for some testing.

Take it slow. There's no need to hurry.

She was yanked back into her physical body with a suddenness that took away her breath. All around her, everything was white and spotless and metallic and clean, more unreal in its sharpness than anything she'd experienced.

She was being disassembled, reassembled—her thoughts were crystal clear.

She looked down at her left arm, flaps folded apart like in some medical demonstration, skin flayed. She felt no horror, no apprehension, but no detachment either; she was there, in the moment, and the moment was there for her.

Someone was monitoring her mind from up close. She reassured the person, and the person reassured her in kind. She felt a vague urge to merge, but instead she floated, floated high, drifted away . . .

I'd say she needs a break, one of the voices said, and she wished to respond that everything was all right, but then there was no more of her and no more of the voice.

Oyārun was lying on a hospital bed, all very white and clean and comfortable. She sank into the pillow and the shape-forming mattress. She was tired like generations, her body heavy as stone in a bed of white fluff, in a white room, completely surrounded, wrapped in a thick blanket . . . was it all really so white, or had her mind stopped making sense of her surroundings altogether? Was it only a simulation or a mindscape?

Either way, she relished the soft sensation all over her body—calming, relaxing, peaceful. Her skin felt raw, chiseled away until it was the thinnest film covering her self.

She made an attempt to tilt her head—so hard. Her skull felt filled with sharp-edged objects, sliding on each other.

Her left arm was lying on top of the blanket. She was wearing a long-sleeved shirt of some sort. Her skin looked unchanged. She tried her hardest to lift her hand, but she could only rotate it a little; still, she got a better view. As the muscles in her hand shifted, she noticed the faint lines embedded in the flesh— or was she imagining things?

She sighed a hoary, raspy sigh and relaxed, her body giving up in exhaustion even though she was no longer in pain.

Aramīn was sitting by Oyārun's bedside. Mentally checking some kind of computer readout? He glanced up when he noticed she'd shifted in bed.

"How are you feeling? All the parameters we're monitoring are well within boundaries." He nodded at a corner of the ceiling.

She still felt very weak but no longer heavy as stone. She could speak. "I'm fine," she said with only a modicum of effort.

"Don't overexert yourself." He paused. "It all went very smoothly."

She wanted to laugh, but she could not manage more than a cough. "It didn't feel that smooth to me."

"Trust me, we've seen worse." Did she glimpse a twinkle in his eye? He looked down and ran a hand over his overcoat, even its muted aubergine a burst of color in the bare white room. When he spoke again, his voice was sober. "You are well-suited for this kind of transformation. I'm very satisfied with the results so far."

"You mean, we should've done this sooner?" She fought an urge to grin at him. She felt giddy.

He cleared his throat. "We could've done this sooner, yes. Still, I am satisfied." Again, a pause. "There is attrition at every stage. Every stage you pass is an accomplishment in itself."

She closed her eyes. "I didn't really *do* anything."

"That's precisely the point. You did not offer resistance. It will only get harder."

She thought of all the recordings, the logs in the Oral History Archives, running them through her mind. She finally grinned as the familiarity of the situation dawned on her. "Is this the point where you ask how well I can tolerate pain?"

"You know I only ask that to get a rise out of people." He sounded vaguely entertained, or was she imagining it? She opened her eyes to look at him. Still she wasn't sure.

"To get a rise out of people and to watch for their reactions," she remarked. Watching for his reaction.

"That too." He was unperturbed.

She chuckled.

He leaned back in his chair, stretching. "So tell me, how well can you tolerate pain?"

Oyārun was still slightly unsteady on her feet, her body still slightly unfamiliar. Heavier, but just a little; definitely firmer. She still habitually poked at the implants protruding from her skull, her spinal column. Not enough space to squeeze everything into the body, she surmised. She didn't change the way she tied her headscarf. Some of the protrusions showed, but she didn't particularly mind. She had not ventured outside yet, and she was curious about the looks she would get, if also somewhat intimidated. Admiration mixed with apprehension? Patriotic pride? She could not begin to guess at people's complicated feelings.

Aramīn pushed her to start practicing almost as soon as she could get around unassisted. He came for her, led her into a small room designated for the purpose.

"I've seen the results of the tests, but let's just do another round," he said in a way that sounded oddly measured, even from him. He instructed her to raise māwal, focus it in specific parts of the body, outside the body. She complied. What was he getting at? Her apprehension grew, even though everything he asked for she could do with ease and with a smoothness that surprised even her. Maybe this really is my path, she thought. She was caught up in the routine, at home within it, fitting in.

He came to an abrupt halt, fell silent. "I should've tried to get a rise out of you," he said quietly.

She blinked at him, feeling her eyes grow large. "Yes?" What was he getting at?

"There are many kinds of pain," he said, his words cautious, feeling their way ahead. "Most we can decrease, manage. But there is a kind of pain that is tied to the essence of the self, and that's intractable to medical manipulations. It's tied to the māwal, and . . ." He looked down at the mats covering the floor with no gap between them, fitting together like puzzle pieces. "The only way is to simply get used to it. Nothing else can be done. It cannot be minimized."

She didn't understand his distress. "I'm all right with that," she reassured him to no effect.

"Not everyone can get used to it."

"You expect me to fail," she said with forced nonchalance.

"You've done well so far," he said, a trifle too fast. "But even the . . . exercises we can perform do not compare to a live run."

He really did expect her to fail. He thought he'd been too lucky to have her? Things had gone too smoothly so far? She didn't understand. He'd done this so many times before. What was different this time? On occasion, he felt weary to her. Was it the repetition? Was he feeling his age? It puzzled her, and she grew impatient.

"Expectations shape reality," she snapped.

He looked up, stared at her dead on. "Then show me you're stronger than me."

This time she was the first to look away.

She could feel his disappointment—faint but still present. I'll show him, she thought and gritted her teeth.

"We can induce this kind of pain. Gradually at first, as much as this can be done gradually. As we raise the thresholds, we can get more and more māwal throughput. Until you're ready for a live run." He rubbed his face. "As much as people can be ready for a live run. Nobody is."

I will show you, she thought at him with newfound ferocity.

He opened a section of the wall. She could see the equipment stored inside. "You might've noticed that this room was soundproofed."

"Most rooms in the Institute are," she said.

"Exactly." He pulled out a red ring of tape. He opened it, clapped it around his wrist. "We can be explicit about everything. We need not have smoke screens and obfuscation, like in the times of the old seers and magicians. More understanding doesn't break the process."

He walked to one end of the room, opened another segment, and pulled out a tall, thick pole of some sort, almost like a column. He walked with it to the center of the room and began to affix it; there was a shape precut into the mats that he could simply pop out to fix the pole to clamps on the floor below. He twisted and something popped out on top, attached itself to the ceiling. He grabbed the pole and pulled at it strongly. It held.

"I have no wish to humiliate you, to degrade you. I only need to cause you pain. Unlike the people of old, we know this is sufficient. What they did to the Imperial Seers was not only inefficient but actively harmful." He unclasped the ring from his wrist. "This time, I'm going to tie you to the pole." He gestured for her to step closer.

She stepped to the pole, put her back to it, obediently allowed him to tie her hands behind the pole. "The world axis, if you will," he said. "The tree connecting the worlds. Many mythological parallels."

He proceeded to make sure she would not be able to slump and injure herself when her muscles gave in.

"Inisayu's ordeal," she offered weakly.

"Inisayu was hanging from the tree upside down, according to legend. I'd rather not risk popping a blood vessel in the brain. It's still quite soon after surgery." He turned away and went back to the locker behind her. "Before you get carried away, know that I have knives and a whip, and I intend to use them." A sound of cloth on cloth—what was he doing?

When he walked again in front of her, she saw. He'd removed his trademark overcoat. He still wore a richly decorated dark-blue vest over a loose shirt, and implements like knife handles hung from his belt. A harness was also hanging from it, housing what looked like a long, yellow, softly glowing tentacle.

He unclipped a handle from his belt and grabbed it in his palm. A glowing blade—some kind of force field?—sprung from it. She recognized the tool as the one he'd jammed into his palm. His own reaction had been strong enough that it physically hurt her, even though his face had remained impassive. "I can see you remember this," he said.

Her muscles spasmed. Her body remembered it before her mind.

"Yes." He smoothed over her forehead with his free hand. "You definitely recall that." The touch strengthened the memory, and it hurt—

"Focused pain can throw the system off-balance in the desired way. It can overactivate the māwal-raising process . . ." His voice drifted away. "We can try. We will go slowly at first. Allow me to demonstrate. Very slowly at first. I am going to put this into the chest center." He indicated the position in the middle of her chest with a long finger. She knew he could not see the way the māwal flowed throughout her body, but he must've done this so many times it was second nature. He pointed at just the right spot. "Then we can do the other centers, but first I want you to be familiar with the sensation."

She nodded assent. He plunged the blade through her clothing—the force field did not wound, only—

She screamed, strained against the bindings.

"I've pulled it out. That was the lowest setting and only for a moment. We will need to increase both the duration and the amount, slowly but surely."

Her entire torso felt like it was on fire.

"Do you think you can take that for a bit longer?"

Her thoughts clumped together, and her tongue tripped over the sounds she wanted to make.

"Bgh—bh—ah—I think."

"Excellent." Did he sound more satisfied than ever before? "Then let's do it again. Eight seconds, do you think you can take eight seconds?"

She could.

She gasped for air once it was over. Her limbs twitched.

"Once more. Maybe we can try sixteen seconds. I'm counting."

She drew in a deep breath.

"Exhale. If you keep in air, it makes it worse. Try to breathe slowly, evenly. A few breaths before we start . . ."

She exhaled. Inhaled. Exhaled again. Inhaled.

"Good. Not *very* deep, you don't want to hyperventilate. That can come in handy at times, but it can also cause unwanted complications. It's best to be careful."

She nodded.

"I'm starting. One . . . two . . . breathe evenly. Four. Five."

Her entire body was tense like a closed fist. The world narrowed to one burning point in her chest. Her consciousness floated, back and forward, out of sync with her body.

"Eight. Nine."

She could do this. She could do this.

The māwal ran through her in large shudders, the air thickening. She found it harder and harder to breathe. Fire to rend the flesh from the bones.

She could do this. She had to. She struggled to build a balance. She thought she could take this for longer. Not indefinitely but longer. Longer.

"Twelve. Thirteen."

Almost over. Almost over.

"Fourteen. I think you can take more."

She nodded, genuinely believing she could. Aramīn pulled up her chin with one quick and practiced movement, pushed her head against the pole. Her eyes widened in surprise.

Aramīn stabbed another dagger into the middle of her forehead.

Later, she did not even know if she had screamed. The world collapsed around her, the searing yet immaterial flames of the māwal licking at the walls, filling the chamber with a ferocious thundering noise. Everything rushed through her, all at once, and her consciousness blinked out.

When she came to, she was still tied to the pole.

"There, that was doable, wasn't it?"

For a long while, she was unable to respond.

Oyārun was lying on a slab, tied down tight. The right sleeve of her white shirt was rolled up above the elbow.

Aramīn was putting daggers through her right arm, one after another. He kept up the talk.

"The first one goes into the center of the palm. An important location. The second just below the wrist, where the radius and the ulna meet. Another in the middle of the forearm. Yet another in the inner elbow. Remember, it works through fabric, but this time I want you to be able to see the sites."

She was taking short, gasping breaths.

"Good, you are doing good. I'm not going to do anything sudden this time. You've made a lot of progress. It's time to rest."

Tears were streaming down her face.

"This is something you can do for yourself. Just one arm. Either the right or the left. I'm going to take these out and untie you, and then you can try."

She sat up, trembling. Her fingers closed around the handle of the dagger, but without any force, and she dropped it in her lap, wincing even though it was turned off.

Aramīn picked up the dagger, handed it to her again. Calmly, patiently, without any urgency.

She fumbled the catch again. A sob wracked her.

"There's no need to hurry. Take your time."

She managed to hold the blade on the third attempt.

"Good. That's a good first step."

She turned on the field. Pushed the blade into her palm, all the way to the hilt. Her fingers closed around the handle automatically.

"It's not going to come out unless you pull it out. You don't need to worry about it. I can give you another one . . . here. There, I can show you the spot."

He gently guided her hand. "Good, now push."

She did.

"Two more. All right? You could take that when I was doing it."

She nodded, forcing out her words from between clenched teeth. "That was . . . easier."

"Yes, passivity is easier for some people, and that's fine. I'm making you do this for a reason."

She nodded again, her neck muscles painfully spasming. She pushed away the impulse to rub her neck. Two more.

She looked at her arm, the hilts of the four daggers poking upward. She held down her arm with her other hand, tried to steady the shaking. Tried to calm the māwal, reroute the disrupted flow, deal with the excess.

"Great." He praised her so much these days, she thought, but always in such a detached manner. She cradled her arm to herself. It felt like it was becoming a burning white conduit for all the power in the universe. She wasn't sure she could keep this up for much longer.

"Relax. Just a few moments . . . good. Now you can try to remove them. Very slowly. One by one. No rash movements. You know what rash movements lead to, right?"

The inside of her forehead lit up with the memory of an excruciating feeling. She was very, very cautious.

"There. Now you see you have control over the process."

"I-I thought I was supposed to be helpless," she offered. Even her lips felt numb, worn out from stimulus overload.

"You're going to be helpless, that's inevitable. Nothing can persist in the face of the raw stream." He glanced away for a moment. "But it's imperative for you to understand that you do have control, as much as it's possible, even if you are helpless. Even if you are made helpless, you have some measure of control."

He had taken to repeating himself, she thought. Was this some kind of technique too?

"I am going to give you that control. And then I'm going to make you helpless, and you're going to hold on to what you have left. Once this is over and you're standing in that point, nothing of you is going to remain, nothing, except this. This will remain. This will remain."

"Th-the shaking isn't stopping," she said, and he sat next to her, held her trembling body to himself.

"It's going to pass," he said.

She broke down in sobs.

"Shh." He cradled her head in one hand. His touch was unexpectedly soothing. "It's going to pass."

Eventually, it did.

"I'm always worried that one day you're going to just walk out, leave me there when I'm all tied up and the blades are in," Oyārun said as they were preparing for another session. He was busy with the pole—the bottom catches did not want to hold.

"I'm not leaving," he said. "I'm going to be here. Even when you'll have to face the stream, I'm going to be there." The catch finally clicked in place. "I cannot be there in the mind, but I can be there, taking care of you, what of you exists in physical reality." He straightened up, looked at her. "That's going to make it a fraction easier. Just a fraction, but easier."

"Thank you," she offered in a wavering voice, even though she knew he was not doing this for her sake: he was doing it for the sake of success. Or was he?

Her world was the chamber, poles and slabs and circular and rectangular frames and the four walls. Chained to a wall. Tied to a frame.

Sometimes she threw up, sometimes she spat blood. Her blood was no longer red; it was opalescent and colorless.

The floor drank up everything, the stains disappearing at a speed discernible to the naked eye.

The world was a burning tree of fire, and she was chained to the tree and stabbed with knives of ice. The world was a swirling circle of storm clouds, and she was tied to the circle and whipped with lashes of lightning.

She lost control. Over and over again. At times, they had to interrupt—the first time it happened, Aramīn said the wards in the walls wouldn't hold, and she realized there was some kind of māwal technology *inside* the walls, hidden from casual observation, redirecting the excess. She only hoped the walls wouldn't come down one day. Surely Aramīn would not let that happen—he had control over her nervous system, he could shut down her consciousness if the immediate need arose.

"You won't allow me to bring down the Institute, right?" Oyārun was feeling especially discouraged that day.

"Hmm?" Aramīn turned to her. "What do you mean?"

She spread her hands. "There's . . . there's so much destructive power." *In me.* She could not bring herself to finish the sentence, say the words out loud.

"You were not built to destroy," Aramīn said. "You were built to sustain."

Oyārun lifted the whip, a long plastic tentacle, gingerly wrapped it around her lower arm. It didn't have a handle. The pain burned, but it was manageable.

A thought struck her. "With this one, the user can't help to feel pain either."

"Exactly." Aramīn nodded.

She made a little lashing motion, little more than a wave. "But that means . . ." She pursed her lips.

"Yes, I also feel pain when I'm using this one." His face was smooth, unexpressive.

"You don't mind?"

"It is a reminder."

Oyārun was tied to a circle frame, handles sticking out of all the primary and secondary māwal centers of her body. She was breathing slowly, evenly.

"Thirty-two minutes," Aramīn said and put the whip back into its holster. "This will have to be enough."

She grunted, beyond speech.

"If you cannot pass the initial acclimatization in this amount of time, it's over," he said, more abruptly than usual.

Was he afraid?

He began to remove the force field blades quickly, as if urged on by someone else. "I have given you this amount of time, now you have to do something with it."

She stumbled forward as he untied her, her muscles giving. He cradled her, but she felt hesitation in his posture.

"Thank you," she said.

Aramīn stared into her eyes, then something intangible swooshed across his face, and his expression changed. "You're welcome." He helped her to the slab, sat her down on the ground with her back to one side. "May the universe itself forgive me, you're welcome."

III.

1.

There was an entire team standing by.

"Let's go over this once again," Aramīn said. "We need constant high throughput. I know you can induce it, but for the first time, I'm going to override some functions and induce it in you myself. Less room for error. The goal is not the pain. The pain is initially inevitable, but it is not desirable. I have given you the ability to manage it. Your mind will tune into the raw stream of the System, and you are going to acclimatize. You are going to belong, to attach. You will need to learn how to process your new sensory environment, how to interact with it. Avoid your usual patterns. Try not to hold on to things, try not to treat them as conventional objects."

Emien helped him out; she was standing by in case of an emergency that might need a māwalēni. "This cannot be explained; this can only be experienced," she said.

"Yes, thank you," Aramīn nodded. "Any last-minute advice you could offer?"

Emien shrugged. "It's ineffable. I don't think I can say anything about it. Try not to resist it. It resists back."

Oyārun was strapped down, but she could breathe freely. This was the moment she had practiced for, all the time spent in that chamber with its walls drinking up the māwal, its floor drinking up her blood.

"All parameters within nominal range," a tech said, looking up from her instrumentation. "Say the word and it's a go."

Aramīn stepped to her. "Show an Enāyūwē transform." He paused, examining the image with the aid of his interface. "Mmm. Looks neat." He began to pace. "Let me look at the settings . . . I'd prefer a smooth buildup, avoid the exponential. B-W of around five."

Nods around the room.

He turned to Oyārun. "We are ready whenever you are."

"Go ahead," she said, and Aramīn raised a hand—

The māwal rushed up her spine, faster, faster, forced by her systems controlled externally for the time being. She did not mind being taken over in this manner—one less thing to track, to manage, to maintain.

There was more and more. It seemed to her that the room had become transparent, and she could see through everything, even though her eyes were closed.

No pain so far. She was so used to this that her pain threshold was considerably elevated. Yet it did not come as a relief. She'd gotten used to pain to the point that it was comforting, and the lack nagged at her.

"Tell the System they can begin syncing," Aramīn said outside. She was inside looking out, inside her own body, yet her mind was expanding, ballooning outward—

And it was there, the stream of the System, faster and more powerful than anything before, and she struggled not to get swept away.

The waves of power battered at her, and as she tried to pick out individual details, they rushed away from her. It was like sitting on the overhead train that passed just below the canopy and staring out—if she tried to focus her eyes on anything nearby, it would get yanked out of sight, and her eyes would almost hurt from the effort of the tracking.

Everything came *at* her, all at the same time. No rest. No reprieve. She could not hold on to anything. There was always something more, something new and searingly bright and manifold. She could not cram it all into her skull.

She was trying to relax, trying to keep herself from hyperventilating, but it wasn't working. Her fingers were tingling—

"Override the voluntary respiratory control," Aramīn yelled outside. "We cannot risk any more vasoconstriction—"

The systems clamped down on her hard, overrode her pattern of breathing. Momentary respite.

Inside, the stream still ate away at her. How could she ever get used to this? She struggled to no avail. She held on for dear life—

"Let go," Aramīn spoke right next to her body outside, and it took her some time to realize that he was talking to her, firmly, ordering her. "Do not resist. Do *not* resist."

I'm not resisting, she wanted to say as she hung on with tooth and nail. *I'm trying—*

Then, an image of the train hurtling past and her sitting on board, staring out, eyes relaxed and taking in the cramped vista passing by without trying to fixate on any single object.

A change.

A letting go.

Something shifted inside her, and there was no more pain, no more of the onslaught, just ceaseless joy and the smooth motion of coasting along the stream.

She did not remember anything else.

Oyārun was close to tears. "I—I know I was there, and it was beautiful, but I don't remember—I don't remember anything else—" She gestured broadly with her arms.

"The two kinds of sensory environments are absolutely different and ineffable from the point of view of each other," he explained slowly and carefully. "Your self here has little to no access to your memories there, and vice versa, your self there has little access to your memories here."

"But I—"

He went on. "It's a quite extreme version of state-specific recall. We've been through this before."

She looked at him, her eyes pleading, and she would have inwardly shuddered at how she might appear to him, begging thus, had she not been past shame. He had seen her screaming in agony, certain the next moment was going to be the last—and he had always been there for her.

Would he desert her now? Would he fail to help her?

"Is it always like this?" she muttered.

"Eventually there's some cross talk. You remember more. But it's always in the form of vague impressions at most. Relatively few substantial memories carry over."

"It was beautiful—"

"And it's going to remain so, and you're only going to see more of it, not less."

Her face crumpled up. She couldn't help herself. "But I can't remember—"

"You remember a little. And what you remember is beautiful." He drew back from her. "Is that not so?"

She lowered her head. "It's true. But I—" She couldn't find the words.

"You crave it."

She looked up, surprised. Did he know her better than herself? Of course, she reminded herself, he'd seen this over and over. He'd seen many people go through this when they joined the System.

"I crave it!" She threw her words in his face. He did not flinch. "I crave it and I need it and I—" She was shaking, not with the māwal but with desperation. Was there a difference? Power crested in her.

"Shh." He drew her to himself. She sniffled into his overcoat. "And you will receive it. Perpetuate it. It's yours."

And yet behind his words was the awareness of time ticking down, of life ebbing away. The transformation shortened the life span. Everything had a price.

She clutched him and shook with tears.

"The first time it took us two days to get you back to your baseline state—after just an hour of being in the System. Expect the same this time around as well. It takes a long time to work up to the norms."

"It's all right," Oyārun said, resigned. She was bone weary, more despondent than exhausted. "I'm sorry."

Aramīn remained silent, but he beheld her with a quizzical expression.

"You were right. About every single thing you've ever told me."

He didn't say, *I told you so.* He didn't even think of it—she could tell. He looked at her with sadness, or only exhaustion? Probably the latter, Oyārun decided. "Do you regret your choice now?"

"No," she whispered. "No, and that's the worst part of it."

He sat down heavily. "Hate me. I can be easily hated. After all, I am generally considered a monster."

"You're not."

"Hm?" Was that actually unpleasant news to him, Oyārun wondered—did he want to be regarded as a monster?

"I've read the testimonials of your coworkers. In the Oral History Archives. Did you know . . ." She felt too tired to speak. "The closer someone was to you during the War of Independence, the more likely they were to speak highly of you."

He leaned forward slightly. "You ran correlations on *that*?" Then he shook his head. "You shouldn't have chosen this path. You should've chosen something . . . anything else."

"This was what I wanted. It's not negotiable."

"Not any longer definitely. Even if you were to walk away from the System, the transformation is irreversible."

Silence.

Aramīn spoke up first. "You're only going to grow farther away from me. You went through your transformation, and I helped you go through it, but my task is done for the most part. I taught you what I could. I try to keep an eye on everyone, check in from time to time, but that's basically it." He spread his hands. "My time is finite." Was he pushing her away? Some part of him was, she decided. But was that the entirety of him?

"I can pray with you," she offered.

Aramīn startled for once. "Excuse me?"

She tried to backpedal. "Or just listen to you praying. I find it beautiful." She swallowed, something uncomfortable occurring to her. "Will you pray for me too? Once I'm gone?" *I will leave this world before you.*

He understood the implications. "I can. I definitely can." He bowed his head formally—in the new Ereni manner, she realized. "I take solace in the fact that you desire that."

2.

They strode along the snaking, winding corridors of the industrial area surrounding Memorial Park.

"So how are you faring? The reports only say everything is in order, but they cannot tell me about how you feel." Aramīn lifted a hand and adjusted his cap just a little. "You're up to the ten-hour limit now."

"Yes, and . . . it's fine. It still takes a bit long to recuperate after my shift. They're telling me that it should go faster . . ."

"I can look at the logs," Aramīn offered. "See if anything jumps out to me, anything that could be adjusted."

"Thank you, that'd be great." Oyārun smiled—a carefree, relaxed smile despite the circles around her eyes. "Otherwise, it's going well."

"And how do you like it?"

"I like it . . ." She paused, took a deep breath. "Let's not try to evade this? Let's be honest. It's vast, it's gigantic, and it's tearing me apart. And despite that, I'm always back for more."

"I'm sorry about that." Was he really? Did she want him to be sorry, at all? "That's the way things are." This much was true.

"I love it. The worst part is the switchover when I realize I'm out, out of the stream, and I want to claw my way back in . . ." Her voice sounded all too loud in the deserted, echoing corridor. "I want to go back. I crave it, every single moment. It never goes away. I can push it back, but it never goes away."

He nodded. "It's not easy, I know." He pulled at his left sleeve to make it look just right. "How much do you actually remember?"

"It's not . . . it's not really *remembering*. But more carries over. It scares me a little. I'm not supposed to be able to do that, and yet . . ." She hesitated. It seemed like too large a thing to say, too large for words. "I've been wondering about it. Maybe it's because I'm . . . maybe it's because I was born planetside? I always had my interface, and that was also very seamless for me. Maybe the two could be combined?"

Aramīn frowned, and in that instant, he appeared more like the scientist he was than ever before. "The planetary computer networks and the System?" He considered it seriously, Oyārun could tell. He was taking her seriously. "Information is information after all. Maybe in a few generations."

Oyārun nodded cheerfully. "They could be combined somehow. I think that would be great. Sometime down along the line."

"Is that you saying that, or is that the System?"

She stopped dead in surprise.

"The connection goes both ways," he said, stopping just a fraction of a second after she did. Always keeping an eye on her. "The influence goes both ways."

"I . . . you're right." She massaged her face. "I don't know." She lowered her hands and looked at him, entirely clueless. "I don't know." Then a torrent of words poured out: "How much of me is me? It's inside me, but I'm also inside it, I help make it what it is, and it also makes me into what I am, and I—"

"Shh. I know. Let's walk."

She obediently fell into pace next to him.

"I have been suspecting that the System is trying to pass me messages," he said. "I get small signals. My environment changing in subtle ways. Trees dropping their leaves, lights flickering when I pass by. People blurting out sentences they themselves cannot explain. The way the māwal is supposed to operate. A lot depends on the carrier. With most people, complex information just doesn't make it across. So far, all I had were fragments, but now some of them at least have fallen into a pattern. A pattern I can understand," he emphasized, and there was something in his voice that for a moment did not bridge the gap between the two of them.

"A pattern you can understand?" she asked, uncomprehending.

"I can understand the hunger to control." There, a piece of the puzzle she'd been looking for. Right there. "I can understand the hunger to expand."

"It's . . . shaped by us, but in turn, it's shaped by you," she offered weakly.

"What do you mean?"

"Indirectly. We are affected by you because you trained us, and we are in the System, so it makes sense . . . for the System to be affected by you." Your cognotype: the words remained unspoken.

He laughed all of a sudden, his laughter shrill and sharp as knives. Like the crack of a whip. "By me? Oh yes! A thousand times yes! But it makes perfect sense—oh, the irony!"

She thought back on the Archive logs. *People will say he is a sadist and a Falconer . . . some of that is true.* And him saying, *I suppose I do have those tendencies,* nonchalant, even satisfied.

He quieted down abruptly. His brow furrowed. "Are you bothered by this?"

She considered it for a moment. "The System is standing between here and the abyss." She closed her eyes briefly. "I have seen the monsters. Some of me has. Inside."

"I know."

"What you're doing . . . it's necessary. I understand that."

"But do you understand the implications?" Again, the old debate. This time about a different topic, but the patterns were the same. "Maybe the way this country will turn out will make people wish it had not come into existence in the first place. Maybe people will curse Eren for centuries to come."

"Do you really think that?"

"I hope that's not going to be the case. But I don't know."

"There's more of us than there is of you," she said. With some of his merciless nature inside her.

He stifled another laugh. "Indeed."

The corridor opened to the familiar cavern. A gust of air caught at their clothing, made Aramīn's overcoat billow, deposited a large leaf on the top of his cap. A sign? A gesture from the System?

Aramīn removed the leaf and turned it around in his hands. He was about to tuck it into a pocket but changed his mind and handed it to Oyārun.

"Well then," Aramīn said, "let us pray."

CONTENT NOTICES

Bolded stories are emotionally heavier reads in general:

- ❖ **"Four-Point Affective Calibration": Discrimination, violence**
- ❖ "An Errant Holy Spark": Violence
- ❖ "And I Entreated": Cissexism, minor mention of bodily harm
- ❖ **"Folded Into Tendril and Leaf": Bodily harm, warfare, imprisonment, self-injury**
- ❖ "The Third Extension": —
- ❖ **"On Good Friday the Raven Washes its Young": Violence, street harassment, intersexism, cissexism, colonialism, destruction of the environment, harm to animals**
- ❖ "Volatile Patterns": Bodily harm
- ❖ "The Ladybug, in Flight": Minor mention of bodily harm
- ❖ "The 1st Interspecies Solidarity Fair and Parade": Bodily harm, minor mentions of cissexism, antisemitism, classism
- ❖ **"A Technical Term, Like Privilege": Bodily harm, body horror, blood, cissexism, classism**
- ❖ **"Power to Yield": Sadism, bodily harm, ableism, death/mourning, brief mentions of warfare**

BONUS NOTES

"Four-Point Affective Calibration"
A lot of this story is based on my experiences living in a university town in Kansas. I actually like living there! But some things need to be said.

I wrote this piece after someone told me my writing about immigration included too much anger and not enough other emotions. Here! Have all the emotions! This will not make anything easier.

"An Errant Holy Spark"
I wrote this story for an anthology focusing on creators of artificial intelligence who are not men. There are multiple creators of different genders in the story who are not men, and of course, artificial intelligences also create themselves.

"And I Entreated"
This one was written for a benefit project, focusing on queer religious themes in SFF. Here I don't problematize the fact that some of the characters are counterintelligence officers, but I have a completed webserial written for Broken Eye Books titled *Song of Spores* set in the same continuity where that forms the main plot.

I also don't problematize that many of the Jewish religious texts that talk about gender/sex nonconformity would be more accurately labeled as intersex texts rather than as trans ones; I do believe these works also speak to non-intersex trans people, and the characters will discover both in the course of their study. However, I do have my feelings about intersex erasure in all historical contexts, including Jewish ones, and hope to be writing about that separately elsewhere. In any case, the immediately following story has an intersex protagonist.

"Folded into Tendril and Leaf"

I really wanted to write a longer story from two perspectives where the following things can both be shown: an intersex person being loved and desired, and the intersex person's own perspective on this.

Separately, I also wanted to write about someone turned into a tree and then just abandoned there due to political upheaval. But I had recently written another story about turning into a houseplant, and a tree felt a bit too conventional after that. So I chose the water caltrop as a more interesting plant, and several of its characteristics also drive the plot. I last picked water caltrops from a boat as a child, back before the plant acquired protected status in Hungary.

"The Third Extension"

Another piece inspired by living in Kansas, it was published at least twice as prose poetry, and it's kind of an in-between work, but I do feel it also belongs here as prose fiction.

"On Good Friday the Raven Washes Its Young"

I wanted to make sure this story about street harassment and violence affecting a young intersex person is ordered after the one focusing more on love, though this story is also about kinship and solidarity and has a hopeful ending.

"Volatile Patterns"

This story is set in my Eren continuity, and I've written about these characters elsewhere too. This is a standalone adventure that was inspired by a table runner that looked essentially identical to a Jewish prayer shawl.

"The Ladybug, in Flight"

This flash story was commissioned by one of my Patreon backers, Alexandra

Erin, about a ladybug and a spaceship or possibly both. Some of the odd science factoids are real actual science factoids.

"The 1st Interspecies Solidarity Fair and Parade"

Győr has yet to hold a Pride parade, and I hope my story will be proven wrong and it can take place before the alien invasion.

This novelette is a sequel to my story "Given Sufficient Desperation" from the anthology *Defying Doomsday*; it has also been reprinted online and podcast by Escape Pod, or you can read it in my previous collection, *The Trans Space Octopus Congregation*. The two pieces share a protagonist, but a lot of time elapses between them, and each can be read standalone. I haven't written more in this continuity yet, but it's tempting—I am intrigued by the difficulties of cooperation between sentient beings of different species, when it is hard enough to cooperate within the same species.

"A Technical Term, Like Privilege"

A rental did *not* drink my blood, but I did live in one that started to collapse, and that probably shows here too.

I always feel like not enough stories about blood magic discuss iron deficiency anemia.

"Power to Yield"

This novella involves a considerable amount of asexual BDSM, especially sadism. It also investigates other heavy topics, like ableism between groups of differently neurodivergent people. The usual term for that would be "lateral ableism," but here it's not exactly "lateral" because there is a power differential involved. I don't think "diagonal ableism" exists as a term, but maybe I can coin it . . .

This story also features people genuinely trying their hardest in difficult circumstances, even if what they ultimately end up doing is imperfect.

PUBLICATION HISTORY

"Four-Point Affective Calibration" originally appeared in *Lightspeed* #93, February 2018 (ed. John Joseph Adams).

"An Errant Holy Spark" originally appeared in the anthology *Mother of Invention*, 2018 (eds. Rivqa Rafael and Tansy Rayner Roberts).

"And I Entreated" originally appeared in the anthology *Keep Faith*, 2019 (ed. Gabriela Martins).

"Folded into Tendril and Leaf" originally appeared in the anthology *Xenocultivars*, 2022 (eds. Isabela Olivieira and Jed Sabin).

"The Third Extension" originally appeared in *Grievous Angel*, September 2017 (ed. Charles Christian).

"On Good Friday the Raven Washes Its Young" originally appeared in *Fireside Magazine*, April 2018 (ed. Julia Rios).

"Volatile Patterns" originally appeared in the Gender Diverse Pronouns special issue of *Capricious*, 2018 (ed. A.C. Buchanan).

"The Ladybug, in Flight" originally appeared on the author's Patreon, commissioned by Alexandra Erin.

"The First Interspecies Solidarity Fair and Parade" originally appeared in the anthology *Rebuilding Tomorrow*, 2020 (ed. Tsana Dolichva); it was also reprinted in *The Best Science Fiction of the Year, Volume 6* (ed. Neil Clarke).

"A Technical Term, Like Privilege" originally appeared in the anthology *Whether*

Change (eds. Scott Gable and C. Dombrowski); it was also reprinted in *We Are Here: The Best Queer Speculative Fiction 2021* (eds. L.D. Lewis and Charles Payseur).

"Power to Yield" originally appeared in *Clarkesworld* #166, July 2020 (ed. Neil Clarke).

ACKNOWLEDGEMENTS

Thank you to my family—my spouse R.B. Lemberg and our teen Mati. I could only write these stories with you in my life! Also my relatives: Mom, Marci, Grandma, Dad, Magdi, Michael, and everyone else. Cheers to my cousin Lackó, keep on creating! All of you, please stay safe out there.

Thank yous to those near and far who provided friendship, commiseration, commentary, or some good books to read: Ada Hoffmann, Ádám Dobay, Aliette de Bodard, Andi C. Buchanan, Ash Maiko Jiménez, Balázs Farkas, Bryn Greenwood, Carrie Caine, Charlie Jane Anders, Charles Payseur, Csilla Kleinheincz, Grace Grey, Hannah Stern, Izzy Wasserstein, Jacqueline Flay, Jill Seidenstein, José Jiménez, Kathryn Schild, Krisztina Timár, Lisa M. Bradley, Liz Derrington, Malka Older, Maura Curran, Nibedita Sen, Nino Cipri, Nóra Selmeczi, Orrin Grey, Polenth Blake, Rasha Abdulhadi, Rivers Solomon, Sam Brody, Sandstone, Shweta Narayan, Sonia Sulaiman, Suzanne Walker, Tina Connolly, Tom Robert, Via Farkas, and Vitaly Chernetsky. I am also grateful to my Patreon backers, without whose support I probably would not have been able to continue writing, especially during the ongoing pandemic.

Thank you to the original editors of the stories and also those who chose to reprint them: Andi C. Buchanan, C. Dombrowski, Charles Christian, Charles Payseur, Gabriela Martins, Isabela Olivieira, Jed Sabin, John Joseph Adams, Julia Rios, L.D. Lewis, Neil Clarke, Rivqa Rafael, Scott Gable, Tansy Rayner

Roberts, and Tsana Dolichva. I am really grateful for your comments and your support. Thank you also to Alexandra Erin for commissioning a flash piece that appears in this book.

I was finishing my dissertation while working on these stories; this would not have been possible if not for the following awesome people. First and foremost, I am grateful to everyone who participated in my dissertation studies. Thank you for doing my strange language tasks! Holly Storkel and Karla McGregor took turns to advise me, and Nichole Eden helped with all manner of details. Suma Suswaram (friend, impromptu office mate, and coauthor of research papers!), Samantha Ghali, Romaric Keuwo, Teresa Girolamo, and all the good people of the KU Student Equity & Inclusion Workgroup cheered me up and made sure I remained alive. (Sam, that sentence you said about sample sizes, that saved my soul.) It was also a pleasure to collaborate with Maliah Wilkinson, and I'm hoping to continue this in the future! While I was feeling desperate of everything, Giselle Anatol, Jason Baltazar and the whole SFF reading group at KU CSSF made me feel that I belonged. Special thanks to Kent Smith and his art class for a place that had absolutely nothing to do with my dissertation.

While working on these pieces, I was also applying for US citizenship and simultaneously trying to avoid being deported by a different branch of the government (it's a long story, to be told elsewhere, G-d willing). My immigration lawyer David Treviño helped ensure I could stay in the country, and the Lawrence Jewish Community Congregation supported our family in our appeal. I am also grateful to the people who wrote letters in support; they are listed above. I am eternally grateful to Kathryn for contributing substantially to my legal fees and to many others who provided smaller sums.

I wrote these stories in Lawrence, Kansas, on the traditional lands of the Kanza and Osage people; over five thousand miles from the place where I was born. As a migrant, I am always aware of the privilege of being able to stay in a place many other people were forcibly removed from, or coercively brought to, by colonizers. Nowadays, Lawrence is home to people from many Indigenous nations, also due to the presence of Haskell Indian Nations University, and to many Black people, people of color, and non-Western people, some of whom have fled from oppression in their countries of origin. I always seek not only to be aware of injustice and inequality but to actively work on dismantling it, and I urge everyone else to do the same.

§

Bogi Takács is a Hungarian Jewish agender trans person (e/em/eir/ emself or they pronouns) and an immigrant to the US. Bogi lives in Lawrence, Kansas, with eir family and a congregation of books. Bogi writes, edits, and reviews speculative fiction and poetry. E is a winner of the Lambda Literary award for editing *Transcendent 2: The Year's Best Transgender Speculative Fiction*, the Hugo award for Best Fan Writer, and a finalist for the Ignyte award, the Locus award, and the Hexa award for advocates of Hungarian SFF. Bogi talks about books at www.bogireadstheworld.com, and you can also find em as @bogiperson on various social media websites.

BROKEN EYE BOOKS

Sign up for our newsletter at
www.brokeneyebooks.com

Welcome to Broken Eye Books! Our goal is to bring you the weird and funky that you just can't get anywhere else. We want to create books that blend genres and break expectations. We want stories with fascinating characters and forward-thinking ideas. We want to keep exploring and celebrating the joy of storytelling.

If you want to help us and all the authors and artists that are part of our projects, please leave a review for this book! Every single review will help this title get noticed by someone who might not have seen it otherwise.

And stay tuned because we've got more coming . . .

OUR BOOKS

The Hole Behind Midnight, by Clinton J. Boomer
Crooked, by Richard Pett
Scourge of the Realm, by Erik Scott de Bie
Izanami's Choice, by Adam Heine
Pretty Marys All in a Row, by Gwendolyn Kiste
The Great Faerie Strike, by Spencer Ellsworth
Catfish Lullaby, by A.C. Wise
Busted Synapses, by Erica L. Satifka
Boneset & Feathers, by Gwendolyn Kiste
Alphabet of Lightning, by Edward Morris
The Obsecration, by Matthew M. Bartlett

COLLECTIONS
Royden Poole's Field Guide to the 25th Hour, by Clinton J. Boomer
Team Murderhobo: Assemble, by Clinton J. Boomer
Who Lost, I Found: Stories, by Eden Royce
Power to Yield and Other Stories, by Bogi Takács

ANTHOLOGIES
(edited by Scott Gable & C. Dombrowski)
By Faerie Light: Tales of the Fair Folk
Ghost in the Cogs: Steam-Powered Ghost Stories
Tomorrow's Cthulhu: Stories at the Dawn of Posthumanity
Ride the Star Wind: Cthulhu, Space Opera, and the Cosmic Weird
Welcome to Miskatonic University: Fantastically Weird Tales of Campus Life
It Came from Miskatonic University: Weirdly Fantastical Tales of Campus Life
Nowhereville: Weird Is Other People
Cooties Shot Required: There Are Things You Must Know
Whether Change: The Revolution Will Be Weird

Stay weird.
Read books.
Repeat.

brokeneyebooks.com
twitter.com/brokeneyebooks
facebook.com/brokeneyebooks
instagram.com/brokeneyebooks